# Ancient Legacies Unleashed

By

Alan Beske

This book is a work of fiction. Most places, events, and situations in this story are purely fictional. Any resemblance to actual persons, living or dead, is coincidental.

© 2003 by Alan Beske. All rights reserved.

No part of this book may be reproduced, stored in a retrieval system, or transmitted by any means, electronic, mechanical, photocopying, recording, or otherwise, without written permission from the author.

ISBN: 1-4107-6165-7 (e-book)
ISBN: 1-4107-6166-5 (Paperback)
ISBN: 1-4107-6167-3 (Dust Jacket)

Library of Congress Control Number: 2003093655

This book is printed on acid free paper.

Printed in the United States of America
Bloomington, IN

Copies of this book may be purchased by
phone or on-line from
1st Books Library

1-888-280-7715

www.1stbooks.com

1stBooks – rev. 10/16/03

For Jayne, Heather, Shannon, and Melissa

# Lanier Library East

## Acknowledgements

Many people helped me bring this, my first novel, to a successful conclusion and I'm grateful for their support and encouragement.

While they are from distant generations past, I'm especially indebted to Homer, Aeschylus, Herodotus, and Thucydides for preserving priceless insights into the awesome ancient Greek culture which would have been lost to the world without their superb efforts at recording the events of their era. Likewise, Dante helped me realize how the legacies of the Greeks have affected our lives over the centuries.

The members of the Big Canoe Writers Group, particularly Joe Satterfield and Fred Shaw, have provided much valuable advice from the beginning of this project, and steered me in the right direction at an early stage.

Others, including Sue Carpenter, Sylvia Isikoff, Jerry Kershner, Charley Nix, Alice Quandt, Jose and Liliana Rodriguez, Luis and Barbara Rodriguez, and Rick and Cindy Williams reviewed an early draft and offered helpful feedback.

Technical advice concerning firearms was given to me by Frank Wood and his associates and I'm thankful for the courtesies they extended to me.

Finally, my strongest support and best advice came from my wife Jayne and daughters Heather, Shannon and Melissa. The girls gave me good insights into the world of modern-day college students and Jayne's suggestions, patience and encouragement were invaluable.

# **Prologue**

*He never doubted his psychological capability to murder, nor his physical capability to perform the executions. Lack of self-confidence had never been a concern of his. Once he set his mind to something, and applied his full concentration to a critical task, he had always been satisfied with the results. He took pride in that.*

*He was also reasonably confident he would never be caught if he decided to end the existence of the four tormentors, although, if he was caught and imprisoned or subjected to lethal injection for his crimes, he could accept that. He would try to avoid capture and would not tolerate anyone who became a threat. But, he did not have an intense fear of imprisonment or death. If he had to pay that price, so be it.*

*No, it was not psychological, physical, or fear of retribution considerations which delayed his decision. It was an intellectual issue with him. Just murdering people using conventional methods had no appeal. Any assassin could do that. So, he did not seriously think about becoming a murderer until he managed to craft execution scenarios which were sufficiently ingenious and enigmatic.*

*Now, the waiting was over. He had reviewed and refined his action plan. It was good. Very good. He was pleased with himself as he enjoyed the expensive cigar he had saved for this moment of celebration.*

*The planning was complete. Now, the exciting part. The action. His first victim would soon depart this earth.*

# **One**

 Have you ever watched and heard a person die, while blood oozed from his mouth and from bullet holes in his chest, as he gasped his final painful breaths through a perforated windpipe?
 When I'm lying in the dark in bed at night with my eyes closed, and there is nothing to distract me, I can see the red blood flowing, like hot lava, and can hear his hopeless raspy gasps. I can even smell the gun smoke and my own sweat if I concentrate hard enough.
 If you haven't witnessed such a horrifying event yourself, was there some other excruciating experience which shattered your youthful innocence and catapulted you into the full reality of adulthood?
 My life-altering episode occurred just two months ago, and I have yet to reach my nineteenth birthday.

 It all began when I arrived in Atlanta to begin my college experience. I was full of excitement and anticipation and anxious to start this next phase of my life. I expected to be challenged by many things as a beginning freshman, but had no way of foreseeing that, before the end of my second semester, I would be drawn into a succession of murders, culminating in the gruesome death which still haunts me.

 My first class, History of Western Civilization, began at ten o'clock on a hot and humid Wednesday morning in late August. I took two wrong turns before finding the classroom, but managed to slide into a seat just before Dr. James Chambers entered. He looked like a model from an up-scale clothing commercial with his wavy brown hair and angular face. He was wearing a lightweight blue blazer which fit perfectly over a white golf shirt and well-pressed khaki pants. He appeared to be a little over six feet and stood confidently as he neatly printed his name, e-mail address, phone number, office location and office hours on the white board at the front of the room.

There seemed to be about forty students in the class. Sunlight streamed in through the bank of large windows on my left, creating the illusion of warmth in the colorless classroom. The concrete block walls were painted beige and the tile floor was a milk-chocolate brown. A world map and a map of the Middle East were pulled down from their holders like old-fashioned window shades and covered parts of the white board. The room certainly wouldn't have won any interior design awards, but I liked the feel of it.

Professor Chambers strode closer to the students in the front row, smiled warmly and paused. The soft sounds of murmuring voices and shuffling backpacks ceased in anticipation of his next move.

He opened the class by introducing himself and describing how he intended to teach the course. He stressed that he encouraged active participation from all students and hoped to get to know all of us personally before the end of the semester.

His relaxed voice had a richness that put me at ease immediately. It was as if he was addressing us as peers, but the words he used, and the subtle authority he generated, left no doubt he was the professor and we were the students.

"If you remember nothing else from what I say today, please remember this," Dr Chambers said slowly and deliberately as he scanned our faces making eye contact with me and most of the other students. "The legacies left by past civilizations aid the learned person in solving the problems of today and tomorrow."

He delivered these words in such a convincing fashion I can still quote them today. I also know now just how true his words really were, especially with respect to the legacies of the ancient Greeks.

During the rest of the class period, Dr. Chambers outlined the topics we would be covering as the semester progressed. We would first learn about prehistory and human development prior to the dawn of early civilizations. We would then cover the ancient Mesopotamian, Egyptian, Greek and Roman civilizations and their influence on Western civilization. After that, we would study the subsequent influences through the centuries up to modern times.

Professor Chambers explained that his specialty was ancient Greece, and, therefore, we would pay particular attention to that important civilization during the first part of the semester. I was glad to hear that since I wanted to learn more about the Greeks.

As the class adjourned, a girl with long blond hair seated to my right leaned closer to me and said, "He's pretty amazing. I didn't have anyone like him in high school. What do you think?"

"He really gets your attention," I responded as I caught the faint aroma of her alluring perfume.

"That's for sure. I'm Sarah Flemming," she said in a mild southern accent with a warm smile.

"Hi, I'm Ryan Anderson," I answered while noticing her bright blue eyes and striking face. Her beauty was beyond that of any of the girls I'd ever met.

"Ryan…Ryan…What a nice name. I like the sound of it. It's so…earthy. Well, I'm off to the book store to get a few things. See you on Friday, Ryan," she said as she rose gracefully from her chair, giving me a subtle smile before she turned and slowly walked away.

"Okay, see you then," I responded, realizing I definitely wanted to get to know her better. She was wearing shorts and I noticed a long scar on her left thigh as she left the room. Her legs were awesome, except for that unfortunate blemish. She seemed to have a slight limp, but I couldn't be sure.

I left the classroom and walked down the front steps of Franklin Hall to the tree-draped central mall of the campus. I sat down on a wooden bench to relax and collect my thoughts before my next class. Here I was, a beginning freshman, and had just completed my first college class. I felt energized and was glad to be at Chancellor University.

I'd been accepted at some other top schools, but Chancellor was my first choice. It was noted for its strong history department, which appealed to me since that was my planned major. Also, I was attracted to the school because of its stately campus and location in a warm climate. I was looking forward to a break from the harsh Wisconsin winters I'd lived with all my life.

School had always been interesting for me, and I'd looked forward to the start of classes each fall. But, this was really special for me since college was likely to offer some completely new experiences.

I hadn't gotten to know many people yet, but had good first impressions of Sarah Flemming and the students I'd met in my dorm since I moved in three days earlier. And I hoped I could locate some of the friends I had made at orientation in June.

After devouring a granola bar and some crackers from my backpack, I attended my two other Monday-Wednesday-Friday classes which were English composition and U.S. history. My English professor, Jean Wilkens, was warm and animated, but my U.S. history professor, Herbert Costanza, seemed gruff and impatient and made me feel uneasy.

The next day I attended my Tuesday-Thursday classes, which were introductory courses in psychology and world literature. It seemed like they would both be okay.

## **Two**

    I arrived at Dr. Chambers' Friday class a few minutes early hoping to again sit by Sarah. While she wasn't there yet, I recognized the girl in front of me since I'd seen her from a distance in my U.S. history class.
    I leaned forward and said, "Excuse me." She turned to face me and I continued, "Hi, we're both in the same U.S. history class. I'm Ryan Anderson,"
    "I thought you seemed familiar," she replied, smiling, "I'm Rebecca Chan."
    "Nice meeting you, Rebecca," I replied. "How'd you like professor Costanza compared with professor Chambers?" As I spoke, I was struck by her dark eyes and silky black hair.
    Rebecca raised her eyebrows and said, "Costanza's a little scary, but Chambers looks good."
    She looked exotic to me, perhaps because I had never met anyone of Asian ancestry before. My small home town was full of Caucasians whose ancestors came from Northern Europe, but other ethnic groups were essentially not represented.
    I hoped that she hadn't noticed my staring at her and replied, "I agree on both counts."
    "I heard students voted Chambers as one of the favorite professors on campus last year, so we may be in for a treat."
    "Let's hope so," I responded.
    "Ryan, you have a cute face. You're not some kind of celebrity are you?"

"Hardly. I'm just a common guy, but thanks for the compliment."

"Sure."

"Nobody could accuse you of being bashful," I replied, smiling.

As I finished speaking, Sarah walked in and sat to my right.

"Morning, Sarah," I said cheerfully.

"What's up, Ryan? You look ready for action today," Sarah replied.

I said, "Sarah Flemming, this is Rebecca Chan. Rebecca and I are in the same U.S. history class. Sarah and I met here after our first class."

Sarah and Rebecca exchanged greetings as professor Chambers entered the classroom. In his opening remarks he said there were thirty-six of us registered for the class with thirty being freshmen and six being sophomores. I liked the sound of that since I didn't want to compete with a lot of upper classmen in my first semester.

Dr. Chambers then handed out some assigned reading materials and talked about a class project due near the end of the semester. We were to form groups of four students each and give a class presentation on a literary or artistic work from an ancient civilization which has continued to be of importance to Western civilization over the centuries up through the present day.

He then spent the rest of the period discussing the Paleolithic Age, otherwise known as the Old Stone Age, which dates from man's first use of stone tools up until about ten thousand years B.C.

After class, Sarah, Rebecca and I agreed we'd work on the group project together and would find another student to join us once we got to know some other people in the class. We decided to have lunch together since we all had a break until our next classes began at one o'clock.

During lunch, I got to know both girls better. We shared a surprisingly strong interest in history and all expected to major in it. I found that to be quite a coincidence. Rebecca and I had no siblings. Sarah had an older brother who was attending college in Boston. Rebecca was from San Francisco and Sarah was from Atlanta. Rebecca and I had middle class backgrounds and had attended public schools. Sarah was from a wealthy family and had attended a high profile private school in Atlanta.

Rebecca was a skilled archer and had been successful in many competitions. Her parents were high school teachers and divorced when she was in middle school. Her mother taught social studies, and she had become interested in history through her.

Sarah's father was a prominent Atlanta attorney with many political connections. Her mother was an active supporter of charitable and artistic organizations in Atlanta. Sarah knew Atlanta well since she had spent her whole life in the city. She had developed a strong interest in forensic medicine through a part time job with the coroner's office. This started as an internship job while she was a junior in high school and she planned to continue it while in college. Sarah's interest in history grew out of her father's love for history. His undergraduate major had been in history and he had always discussed history topics with Sarah and her brother as they were growing up.

I explained that my father owned a small company which made boating accessories and my mother was an architect. We lived in a rural community in Southwestern Wisconsin. I got interested in history through my high school history club led by one of my favorite teachers. I'd been a jock in high school and could hold my own on the guitar.

We were all freshmen and were still trying to figure out what college was all about. We had some similarities and differences, but we hit it off well with each other.

In English composition, Dr. Wilkens wasted no time in convincing us she would keep us very busy all semester. We got our first writing assignment and a schedule of what we had to look forward to in the weeks ahead. It was going to be a lot of work but, since my writing skills could stand some improvement, that didn't bother me. I felt comfortable with Dr. Wilkens. She seemed to have high standards laced with a sense of humor.

Rebecca and I sat together in Dr. Costanza's class. His clothes and shoes were black and he was completely bald. He looked and talked like a gangster and was intimidating. I was afraid we'd be in for trouble with him.

I talked with Rebecca for a few minutes after class and then walked to the mall. I sat on a bench near a stone sculpture of a boy with his dog and admired it for a few moments. My mother, as a result of her architectural and artistic training, had given me an appreciation for aesthetics and art, particularly sculpture. The artist had given a timeless and serene quality to the images. The two companions were enjoying their play together and it was relaxing just looking at them. I had noticed some similar sculptures at other locations on campus and wondered if any of them were created by the same person.

The sculptures blended tastefully into the beauty of the campus as a whole. The various parts of the campus seemed well planned, almost as if an artist had painted all of the components on a large canvas and then this artistic blueprint had been transformed into reality by architects, builders and landscapers.

All of the buildings on campus had a historic, academic character and integrated well with each other, whether they were older buildings or buildings constructed in recent times. The campus was fairly compact and vehicular traffic was restricted to the perimeter. This resulted in a peaceful environment free of most modern day noises. If there were no students in your field of vision to give you time clues through their clothing and hair styles, and no landscapers were at work, with their contemporary implements, you wouldn't know if you were in the eighteenth or twenty-first century from anything you could see or hear.

The grounds were immaculate throughout the campus. Grassy areas were thick and lush without bare spots or discolorations and were neatly trimmed along walkways. The walkways were strategically placed and I hadn't noticed any dirt paths caused by people taking shortcuts. Some tasteful color was added by various flowers and shrubs.

I especially liked the sights and sounds of the squirrels, birds, and occasional rabbits found throughout the campus. They contributed to the timelessness and serenity of the environment.

The greatest part of the campus, the focal point, was the central mall where I was now sitting. The main library was at one end and the student center was at the other end. Most of the liberal arts and science classrooms and departments were housed in the buildings on the sides of the mall.

I had learned from the view book that Chancellor University was founded in 1870 after the Civil War by a wealthy Southern industrialist who somehow managed to maintain part of his fortune through the war years. He devoted essentially all of his remaining resources and personal energy to the school, which he envisioned as the South's answer to the elite Yankee schools in the Northeast. He felt the South needed a fine educational institution to assist in the physical and psychological rebuilding required after the war.

Following a modest beginning, Chancellor eventually thrived and today enjoys a prestige similar to Vanderbilt and Emory, the two other Southern schools I had researched.

After spending about thirty minutes relaxing on the mall, I went to the library to see if I would be able to check my e-mail using the wireless internet connection system.

We learned in orientation that Chancellor had made a special effort over the past few years to develop a state-of-the-art computerized campus environment. Starting this year, all incoming students were expected to have a laptop computer meeting standards established by the IT department. A key requirement was that the computers were to be configured so they could connect with the internet using the high speed wireless connection systems installed in all dorms, classrooms and libraries. Numerous administrative and academic functions affecting students were performed on line. While some paper was used, there was a heavy reliance on electronic communications between students and faculty members.

My first attempt to use the internet connection was successful. I easily found some material Dr. Wilkens had asked us to read and then read a few e-mails from high school friends attending other schools. I found Sarah's and Rebecca's e-mail addresses in the electronic directory and sent them a quick note to test out the system. Almost immediately I received a reply from Rebecca over the instant messaging system. I responded and wished her a good weekend.

I smiled as I closed my laptop, feeling pleased with myself. My first few classes had gone well and I had already made friends with two intriguing females who seemed to enjoy my company. College life was even better than I had expected. I slipped my computer into my backpack and headed to my dorm.

"Hey, bro," my roommate, Mike Boyer, said as I entered our dorm room. He was a good-natured African American who was on the Chancellor crew team. We had meshed well in the first few days we had known each other, although crew took up much of his time and he was gone a lot.

"Mike, my man, what's happening?"

"You move fast, my friend. I saw you with two foxy ladies around lunch time, but decided to not butt in."

"Oh yeah, what'd ya think of em?"

"Got good taste man…A Southern belle and an exotic temptress…I'm jealous already."

"Not bad, huh?"

"I'm not surprised. With your face and country boy style I doubt you've ever had much trouble attracting women."

"What can I say? You probably do okay yourself."

"Can't complain."

"Anything doing tonight?" I asked hoping for some excitement.

"I'm going to a party with Jay and Dan. What'd ya say?"

Jay Butler and Dan Gomez both seemed a little wild and were in the room across the hall.

"Sounds good to me."

Just then Jay and Dan banged on the door and pushed it open. They were always ready for action and I could tell from the expressions on their faces, tonight was no exception. After a few jokes, we went to an apartment of a senior from Jay's home town where we consumed ample quantities of beer and hot dogs and played poker until Dan won all the money.

We stayed there over night and watched Chancellor lose its first home football game the next day. It was a good contest, but we lost by a field goal in the last thirty seconds.

After the game we went back to the apartment and spent the evening going around to various parties in the complex. Everyone was having a good time despite our frustrating loss in the stadium.

# **Three**

When I got to Dr. Chambers' class ten minutes early on Monday morning, Rebecca and Sarah were already there. As I sat down behind Rebecca with Sarah to my right, I said, "Hi guys...good weekend?"

Sarah yawned and replied "I think my boyfriend is about to become my latest ex-boyfriend."

"Is that, like, a bad thing?" Rebecca asked.

"Not really. After being here for a few days, he looks so juvenile. Besides, there seem to be plenty of guys on campus who could make a girl happy."

"You mean someone like Ryan?" Rebecca chided.

"He's cute enough but we don't know much else about him yet," Sarah said as she smiled at me.

"Okay, you guys need to calm down and pay attention. Here comes Chambers," I responded, frowning at both of them.

"We are going to be spending much time together this semester. And I'm hoping I'll also be having many of you in future classes," Dr. Chambers said. "Therefore I'd like us to get to know each other better. I'll start by telling you a little about myself and then I'll ask each of you to say a few words."

"I've been on the faculty here for the last ten years. As many of you know, Chancellor is noted for having one of the best history departments in the nation. That's what attracted me initially and that's why I hope to be here for a long time to come. Our faculty consists of a stimulating blend of eminent veterans combined with younger scholars who are starting to gain some recognition for their vigor and innovation. Our professors are diverse in terms of their areas of specialization, personalities, cultural backgrounds and research styles. These features are beneficial to our students, especially those who seek undergraduate and graduate history degrees from Chancellor.

"While I teach various courses, my specialty is ancient Greece. I have my father to thank for that. He was a career diplomat and, as a result, I lived and attended schools in Greece, Israel, Italy and the United States before I graduated from high school. That international exposure gave me an interest in history in general and ancient Greece in particular.

"I got my undergraduate degree at Furman and my doctorate at the University of Chicago. Both schools gave me a solid foundation. I came here right after finishing at Chicago. While Chancellor is wonderful, I'm also a big fan of Atlanta and our appealing climate. I don't have a lot of spare time, but try to play pool regularly and golf on rare occasions. Since I'm an academician, as you can imagine, much of what I read can be quite dry and arcane. I don't mind a good dose of that, but on the lighter side, I delve into a good mystery whenever I have a chance.

"Well, that's enough about me," Dr. Chambers concluded. "Let's learn more about the rest of you. I'd appreciate it if the fellow in the green shirt in the corner would start and we'll then work around the room to the young lady in the Chancellor shirt near the door. Please tell us your name, where you're from and one of your special talents you would like us to know about. In the interest of time, please limit your remarks to one minute. Please stand when you make your comments."

The boy in the green shirt said his name was Tyler Sanders and he was from Atlanta. He was neatly dressed in a golf shirt and shorts and gave the impression, just through his appearance, that he was a likable person. He was stocky, and seemed a little older than the other students. He said his special talent was finding unique but logical solutions to difficult problems.

Others students made their comments after Tyler spoke. A pleasant girl, named Laurel Masters from Minneapolis, who was short and slightly plump, caught my attention, partly because, being from

Wisconsin, I felt we had some things in common. She told us she had a special talent for playing the piano and, because of that, planned to major in music.

When Rebecca talked, she said she was from San Francisco and had a special talent with computers, inspired by her uncle who runs a small technology company in Silicon Valley. Her short sleeveless blue top left a thin band of torso exposed above her shorts. I was probably not the only guy in the room who noticed her well-toned figure.

I spoke after Rebecca. I said I was from rural Wisconsin, played the guitar and hoped to form or join a band on campus. I added that I was looking forward to the Atlanta winters and guessed Laurel probably felt the same way since we were almost neighbors up North. She snickered at that remark when I looked in her direction.

When it was Sarah's turn, she had a smile on her face and spoke in her warm drawl. After explaining she was an Atlanta native, she said she had a talent for acting and wanted to perform in a campus play before graduating. There was a subtle mischievousness in her manner when she made this comment. She looked like an actress standing there and I felt she would decisively win the Miss Georgia contest if she ever entered the competition.

We kept going around the room and the rest of the students made their comments. It was a fun exercise which seemed to make us all feel more comfortable with each other. I felt this was a good move on Dr. Chambers' part and was probably an example of why he was such a popular professor.

At the end of class, he thanked us for our comments and asked us to come to our next class prepared to talk about early civilizations in Mesopotamia.

When we were getting up and putting on our backpacks, Laurel Masters walked over to me and said, "Hi, neighbor. I love your accent. Hey, if you need a keyboardist in your group, I'm interested."

"Look who's talking about an accent. Are you serious about getting in a band?"

"Yeah, that would be awesome! Playing classical piano music is great, but I've always wanted to branch out."

"Let's keep in touch on this," I said feeling excited. As the room emptied, I introduced Laurel to Rebecca and Sarah.

That afternoon in English, Dr. Wilkens discussed our principal paper which would be due at the end of the semester. After class I made an appointment to review this with her at eight o'clock the next morning.

Following our U.S. history class, Rebecca and I took a break in the student center and sat on some overstuffed chairs near a large TV set. We both had a lot of work to do, but wanted to relax before hitting the books. I welcomed the chance to spend some time with her.

"As a part of my financial aid package, tomorrow I'll be starting a job working in the campus library system's computer department." Rebecca said.

"What will you be doing?"

"Mainly solving technical problems and working on the library's web site. I'll be working about fifteen hours per week, pretty much at the times I decide to work."

"With all of your technical talents, they'll be glad to have you, I'm sure."

She smiled back and said, "I'll do my best to impress them."

"Are you going to have a chance to keep up with your archery here?"

"I hope so. I brought my equipment and plan to join the archery club."

"Sounds like fun."

"Say, Ryan," she continued, "Where did you get that gorgeous curly blond hair?"

"The curls come from my dad and the color comes from my mom."

"I'm glad you don't cover it with a backward baseball cap. The guys who wear them like that look like tenth graders."

"I wouldn't do that."

We talked for a few more minutes and then Rebecca left. She was going to work out in the fitness center in the field house before tackling her homework. She said she tried to work out several times a week.

I missed my basketball and football conditioning and was getting out of shape. I knew I should work out like Rebecca, but, unfortunately, didn't have her will power.

I stayed in my seat, read for awhile, and then noticed the five o'clock news was starting on a local Atlanta station. I'd been a little isolated since arriving on campus so decided to watch and see what was happening in the world.

With only a few days of the semester behind me, things were about to change.

# **Four**

    The lead story concerned a prominent Atlanta physician, Dr. Peter Mason, who had been missing for the last two days. He and his wife had been spending the weekend at their cabin in the mountains north of Atlanta. He was an avid hiker and she last saw him at eight o'clock on Saturday morning when he left to take a hike on the Appalachian Trail. He had said he would return about six that evening for dinner.

    There was nothing unusual in Dr. Mason's planned hike that day since he regularly took hikes on various trails when they spent weekends at their cabin. On the day of his disappearance, his wife said he had planned to walk alone. He preferred solitary hikes since he liked to enjoy nature and get away from human contact from time-to-time as a stress-relieving experience.

    In concluding the story, the news reporter said Dr. Mason's wife had reported his disappearance to the police on Sunday morning and the case was now under investigation. Police were questioning Mrs. Mason, friends, co-workers and others who may be able to provide helpful information. His car had been found parked beside Georgia Highway 60 where it crosses the Appalachian Trail north of Dahlonega, a town approximately one hour north of Atlanta. A search team was looking for Dr. Mason along the trail near where his car was parked. There were no promising leads at present.

    After the news announcer moved on to a new story, I noticed a headline in the *Atlanta Herald* on the table in front of me which also pertained to Dr. Mason's disappearance. The reporter was listed as

Steve Simmons. The newspaper article provided much the same information as presented in the news broadcast.

The disappearance of Dr. Mason captured my attention since I had an interest in the Appalachian Trail. I knew the trail ran from Maine to Georgia and I had hoped to do some hiking on it while I lived in Atlanta.

I found myself speculating on what could have happened to Dr. Mason. Could he have had a heart attack? Did he meet with foul play? Did he intentionally vanish? Did he hit his head in a fall and lose his memory? There were many possible explanations for his disappearance. I was intrigued by what might have happened to him.

My mind then wandered to my large paper for English. I had to think of a topic before I met with Dr. Wilkens in the morning. What if I did my paper on this missing person case? Maybe, I could work with Steve Simmons or someone else at the *Atlanta Herald* as a form of class assignment under the supervision of Professor Wilkens. The more I thought about it, the more I felt I should raise this idea with her.

I went to the library about eight o'clock after having some pizza with Mike and a couple of guys from my hall. I liked the environment in the library. It was usually quiet, unlike the dorm, and had a comfortable atmosphere.

The large central part of the library had heavy wooden tables and heavy wooden chairs. The chairs had comfortable dark green velvet-like seat cushions. The carpet on the floor seemed to be of excellent quality and had muted oriental patterns. The ceiling was very high and there were some leaded glass windows near the top of the walls.

While some light was provided by ornate overhead fixtures, most of the lighting came from reading lamps with translucent green ceramic shrouds in the centers of the long tables. The tables were surrounded by shelves full of books. There were individual study desks at the ends of the shelves along the outer walls, but I preferred working at the large tables. I liked the lamps on the tables and especially enjoyed sitting under their pools of light when it was dark outside.

We were going to discuss *Agamemnon* in my world literature class in the morning, and I read it straight through. I'm not sure I

## Ancient Legacies Unleashed

absorbed all of the finer points, but I enjoyed the story. I hadn't read a Greek play before and hoped to understand it better after some review in class.

My mind began to wander after finishing the play, and eventually I began to think about the disappearance of Dr. Mason. I decided to see what I could find out about the Appalachian Trail on the internet so I pulled out my laptop. I found a map which showed that the southern terminus of the trail was at Springer Mountain, located north of Atlanta. On the map I noticed that Georgia Highway 60 appeared to cross the trail about ten to fifteen miles northeast of Springer Mountain. I closed my eyes and tried to visualize the trail before I went back to my room.

The next morning I got up early and watched the local news in the student center. Many other students were gathered around the TV set. Dr. Mason was still missing, and there didn't seem to be any new information. It was obvious from the newscast that this had become a big local story and my interest in writing about it was heightened.

After some searching, I found Professor Wilkens' office in the English Department on the third floor of Jefferson Hall. She was on the phone and motioned me in from the open doorway as she continued her conversation. This was the first time I had been in a professor's office, and I was intrigued by what I saw. The room was brightly lit with sunlight through a large window overlooking the mall. There were full book shelves on two walls, diplomas and awards on another wall, and her desk faced the wall to the left of the doorway as you entered the room. There was a large cork board in front of her desk full of pictures, letters, lists, yellow post-it notes and cartoons. Her computer and printer were to the right of her desk.

There was a small round table with two chairs near the wall opposite her desk. The table top was covered with messy piles of colored folders, books and professional journals. The book shelves contained books, reports, magazines, decorative coffee mugs and pictures of dogs, with everything placed or stacked haphazardly. While the office was over-stuffed and not well organized, I enjoyed being there to experience the ambiance of it. I wondered if one could gain any insights into Dr. Wilkens' personality by analyzing her office.

She was still on the phone and laughed at something the other party said. I sat down by the table to wait. Dr. Wilkens had her blond hair pulled into a pony tail. If you looked closely at her face, and noticed the subtle wrinkles, she seemed to be about forty. From a distance, however, she hardly looked old enough to be a professor.

She had motioned to me a couple of times implying that she would be right with me and I only waited about three minutes before she hung up the phone.

Dr. Wilkens then smiled and said as she walked over to me, "Ryan, I'm sorry to keep you waiting, but that was an old friend from graduate school who called to check up on me."

Then, I was surprised when she removed all of the items from the top of the small table and placed them on the floor before she sat down across from me and said, "Sorry about the mess, but they don't give us much space in these offices. It's crowded, but it's my campus home and I'm fond of it."

I was impressed with how she quickly put me at ease through her actions.

"I always like to get to know my students better and I'm glad you stopped by. Do you want to talk about your long paper?"

"Yes, and thanks for meeting with me on short notice. I have an idea I'd like to discuss with you"

She smiled at me and said, "Okay, let's hear it."

"Last night I saw a TV news report about the missing Atlanta physician, Dr. Peter Mason. I also read about the story in the *Atlanta Herald*. It struck me that there could be many possible reasons behind his disappearance, and, due to his prominent social status, there will probably be much focus on this case, regardless of the outcome. The fact that he apparently disappeared on the Appalachian Trail got me especially interested in the case since I've always wanted to walk on the trail. Have you heard about this story?"

I could see I'd gotten her attention when she responded, "Yes, and by now, most people in Atlanta have heard about it."

"Well, it may not be exactly what you had in mind for our assignment, but I'd like to write my paper about this case as it evolves between now and the end of the semester. Dr. Mason may turn up by then or he may still be missing, but I would like to write about what happens, perhaps from the perspective of a news reporter, if you feel this would be an acceptable approach."

"Ryan, it would be an unconventional approach to the assignment, but it could be a valuable writing experience for you and I'd support the idea."

Maybe it was just my imagination, but she almost seemed to be flirting with me as we talked. She was definitely an attractive woman, but she was probably more than twice my age and she was, after all, my professor. So, while her possible interest in me momentarily got my attention, I decided it best to remain friendly, but not give her any encouragement. This seemed especially wise in case she really wasn't flirting with me.

Anyway, after this quick mental review, I simply said, "Thanks, I'm glad to hear that you approve. Do you have any advice on how I might approach the task?"

She again smiled, and said, "This may be your lucky day. I attended Chancellor as an undergraduate and one of my classmates liked Atlanta so much that he never went back to his home in Texas. His name is Charley White. He got a master's at Georgia State and then went to work at the *Atlanta Herald*. He's been there ever since and is now their human resources manager. I'll bet I could prevail upon him to be of some help to you. We trade favors now and then."

"It would be great if you could ask him to help me. Maybe he could introduce me to the reporters who will be working on the story."

"Okay, Ryan, sit tight while I give Charley a call."

She went to her phone and had Mr. White's assistant get him out of a meeting to take her call. I could tell they were good friends by hearing just her side of the conversation. I ended up with an appointment to meet Mr. White in his office at five o'clock that afternoon. I thanked Dr. Wilkens for her help and got to my psychology class just as it started at nine o'clock.

My mind kept wandering while our teacher was lecturing and I didn't absorb much of what she was saying about psychology. I kept thinking about Peter Mason, Dr. Wilkens and my afternoon meeting with Charley White.

As expected, we discussed *Agamemnon* in my literature class. It's a fascinating story and our professor, Dr. Sandra Chase, led us in a stimulating discussion. The play was based on events following the Trojan War between the Greeks and the Trojans. The war occurred after Paris, a son of the King of Troy, abducted Helen, reputedly the most beautiful woman in the world. Helen, who may have willingly left, was the wife of Menelaus, the king of Sparta. Agamemnon was the most powerful king in Greece. He was Menelaus' brother and was married to Helen's sister Clytemnestra.

Agamemnon led the Greek army which consisted of many powerful Greek leaders including Menelaus, Odysseus, Achilles and others. The army planned to fight the Trojans at Troy to seek revenge for Helen's abduction and bring her back to Greece. However, the Greek fleet was unable to sail due to a lack of favorable winds. Agamemnon learned from a seer that no favorable winds would emerge unless he sacrificed his daughter, Iphigenia, to appease the gods. Agamemnon felt he must go through with this distasteful act and tricked Clytemnestra and Iphigenia in making ready for the sacrifice.

The Greeks got the needed winds for their ships and sailed to Troy where the war took place and lasted for ten years.

In the meantime Clytemnestra never forgave Agamemnon and schemed with her lover, Aegistus, to kill Agamemnon when he returned to Argos. Agamemnon eventually did return after the war and was, in fact, killed by the two conspirators.

## **Five**

    While many students didn't have cars, I was glad I'd been able to bring my aging Chevy Cavalier to Atlanta. I had inherited it from my mom when she upgraded to a newer vehicle. It wasn't modern in any respect, but had always given me dependable service. Since I had already heard many complaints about Atlanta traffic, I allowed myself plenty of time to drive to the Herald using a map from the internet.

    The receptionist let Charley White know I was in the lobby. He met me there and took me to his office.

    "Jean Wilkens is a good friend of mine and it's hard to turn her down when she asks for help. She said you are interested in writing about the Peter Mason case in order to meet a requirement for her composition class," Mr. White said as we sat down in his office. "Since I'm the human resources manager here, I don't get directly involved in news reporting. However I've asked Steve Simmons to join us and he's the lead reporter covering the story. Steve's been with the Herald for over twenty-five years and is an aggressive and respected professional. He also has a mellow core beneath his crusty exterior, once you get to know him. Steve's been at the center of most of the prime stories in Atlanta for a good many years."

    Just then, Steve Simmons walked into the office, and Mr. White said, "Steve Simmons, this is Ryan Anderson. Steve, as I mentioned earlier, Ryan is a student from my friend Jean Wilkens' English comp class at Chancellor. He hopes to do a paper this term on the Peter Mason story. Is there anything you could do to help him out?"

Steve Simmons seemed about sixty years old and was wearing a rumpled gray suit, wrinkled white shirt, and a lose-fitting gaudy blue tie. The only thing missing was a soggy cigar. He looked like a veteran journalist who would tirelessly follow his leads and complete his stories in accordance with the merciless daily deadlines. Steve scanned me from head to foot slowly a couple of times, cleared his throat loudly, squinted and said gruffly, "Have you ever done any news reporting?"

"No I haven't, but I'd welcome anything you could teach me about it," I responded, feeling a little intimidated.

"Well, I've been in this business for a long time and have learned a few things along the way," he replied in a more mellow voice, perhaps sensing my discomfort and trying to put me at ease. "I'll do what I can to enhance your learning experience."

Mr. White looked at Steve and said, "Could you help him specifically regarding his paper about the Peter Mason story?"

"I'll see what I can do. If you don't mind, Charley, I'll take Ryan back to my cubicle for a few minutes and we can discuss how to proceed," Steve said in a commanding manner which left no room for argument from Mr. White, me or anyone else.

"That sounds like a good idea," Mr. White said. "Steve, thanks for your help with this."

Then, looking at me, Mr. White said, "Ryan, I'll leave you in Steve's capable hands. And good luck in Jean's class. She's a fine person and a great teacher."

"I agree. Thanks for all your help," I responded as Steve and I left the office.

We walked through the building and got to Steve's work area. Actually, he shuffled and I walked. He had a cubicle which contained his computer, printer and desk surfaces on two of the walls. He was on the seventh floor and the open side of his cubicle was a few feet from the glass wall of the building. As we were sitting down, I noticed that the interior walls of his work area were covered with newspaper clippings. There were various file folders and papers on the desk surfaces. It looked like a place where a lot of work was done, but things seemed fairly neat and organized, unlike what I would have expected based on Steve's personal appearance.

*Ancient Legacies Unleashed*

"This is where I spend a sizable portion of my waking hours," he said. "It's cramped, but I have a nice view of the city. That's Centennial Olympic Park, one of the enhancements to our city as a result of the 1996 Olympics." As he spoke, Steve's gruffness was replaced with some warmth. He now seemed more like a grandfather than the skeptical scruffy journalist I had seen minutes earlier. I started feeling more relaxed.

"You do have a wonderful view of the park and the city."

"I can tell from your accent you're not from the South. Are you from Minnesota or the Dakotas? You sound a little like the actors in *Fargo*," he said with a faint grin on his face.

"You're close. I'm from Southern Wisconsin, close to the Minnesota border. The actors may have gotten a little over-dramatic with the accents, but they were fairly realistic. I guess I do sound like that."

"Since you're new to Atlanta, does that mean you're a freshman?"

"Yeah. I'm still pretty green."

"Well, I guess we should talk about why you're here today. You want to do a paper on the Mason story. His disappearance is, indeed, a mystery at this point," Steve said as he loosened his tie, more than it already was, and hung his coat on a hook. "All we know is that he just disappeared. He may have been a victim of foul play; he may have vanished voluntarily; he may have been kidnapped; or, maybe there is another explanation."

"How much time will you spend on this story?"

"Probably virtually all of my energy will go into this until key issues are resolved. Depending on how things turn out, this may have a simple outcome or it could be one of the biggest stories we've had in Atlanta in the last several years. It's the type of thing people in my profession love to get their hands on," Steve said with intensity.

"Where do you go from here?"

"Most of it is pretty obvious. I'll be looking at this from various angles and trying to learn what I can from his wife, professional associates, friends, law enforcement personnel, people who are searching for him in the mountains, etc."

"What will you be focusing on initially?"

"I'd like to learn more about the search effort and what clues, if any, are coming out of that. Then, since foul play can't be ruled out, I want to see what he may have been involved with that could have given anyone a motive to harm him. Also, I need to learn much more about Dr. Mason to see if he had any romantic problems or any reasons for staging a disappearance. As you can appreciate, I've got plenty to keep me busy for a while and am going to have to get back to work in a few minutes."

"I understand and appreciate all the time you have spent with me today. In terms of my paper, do you have any suggestions for me?"

"Ryan, I can tell you're a bright boy and I know you wouldn't be a student at Chancellor if you weren't. I encourage you to be resourceful and think and act like a news reporter as you put your paper together. Who knows, you may have a real talent for this sort of thing," he said smiling. "And please keep up with everything I write about the case and what other members of the media are reporting. Finally, feel free to contact me along the way if you'd like to talk about the evolution of the story and your own game plan," he concluded as he stood up and gave me one of his business cards.

"Thanks for seeing me today, Mr. Simmons," I replied as I rose. "I look forward to getting some continued guidance from you. I'll be on my way now so you can get back to work."

"You're welcome, Ryan, and from now on, call me Steve. I'm not one for a lot of formality. Good luck. Give me a call or send me an e-mail when I can be of more help."

In Dr. Chambers' class the next morning we discussed early civilization in the Tigris and Euphrates Rivers region known as Mesopotamia. Professor Chambers led the discussion but, as was his custom, he generated much class participation. We reviewed political, religious and cultural accomplishments of those peoples and learned that some of the earliest civilized cities in the world were probably in this region.

After class, Rebecca, Sarah and I asked Tyler Sanders to join our team for the class project. He seemed very knowledgeable judging from his class participation in our first few sessions and we were anxious to recruit him. Tyler was glad to join up with us, especially when we said we wanted to focus on something about the Greeks. With our team formed, we made an appointment to meet with Dr. Chambers at three o'clock the next day to discuss the project. We decided to meet in the student center thirty minutes in advance to organize our thoughts.

Rebecca, Sarah, and I then had some lunch. The weather was warm and sunny, consistent with the last several days, and we sat in the shade under an oak tree on the mall.

"Have you been following the news reports about Dr. Peter Mason who's missing in the North Georgia mountains?" Sarah asked excitedly. "He and his wife are pretty well known in Atlanta. My mom's a friend of Trina Mason, Dr. Mason's wife. They've worked together on some committees."

"As a matter of fact, I have gotten caught up in the story and plan to write a paper about it for my English composition class," I said. "Dr. Wilkens, my professor, arranged for me to meet with a friend of hers at the *Atlanta Herald* and yesterday he introduced me to their lead reporter on the story. I'll probably be getting some help from him on my paper."

"Cool," Rebecca exclaimed. "I've heard some of the news reports. It sounds like quite a mystery."

"Ryan the reporter…just like Clark Kent," Sarah added. "I'm impressed."

"Thanks," I responded. "Sarah, it's interesting that your mom knows the doctor's wife."

"Yeah, they're pretty good friends and have known each other for a long time. I maybe shouldn't be mentioning this, but, according to my mom, it's fairly well known that Peter and Trina Mason have had some problems with their relationship for awhile. There have been some arguments between them which took place at some high profile charitable gatherings. Also, Trina has told my mother and other women she has suspected her husband of cheating on her on more than one occasion, but she could never prove it."

"It sounds like a soap opera," Rebecca said excitedly, almost spilling her drink in the process. "Maybe Mason's wife or a lover's husband did away with him on the trail."

"Yeah," I said, "or, if Mason felt things were getting too complicated on the romantic front, he may have decided to stage a disappearance and go start a new life somewhere where he wouldn't be found."

"Since we're speculating, what if he was killed by a bear or other wild animal?" Sarah added.

"Are you serious?" Rebecca exclaimed.

"I'm serious, y'all."

"Really?" I said.

Sarah smiled and said, "Actually, like the Masons, my parents have a home in the mountains which we use for weekend breaks, vacations and entertaining. We have some bears in our development and many other wild animals, although only the bears could be a threat to people."

"Well, maybe the missing Dr. Mason was attacked by a bear," I interjected.

Sarah noticed Tyler walk up behind me as I finished talking and said "Hi Tyler, care to join us?"

"Sure," he said. "Are you talking about the missing Dr. Mason?"

"Yes," Rebecca said. "Have you been following the case?"

"Yeah, especially since I know who he is through my part time job. I work for a janitorial service which cleans a medical office building at night and he has his office in that building."

"Do you know him?" Sarah asked.

"Not really. He's been in his personal office a couple of times working late as we started cleaning." Tyler responded, "And I know he drives a red Corvette since I saw him leaving the doctors' section of the parking lot in it as I was coming to work one night."

"That's interesting," I said.

"Hey, thanks for asking me to join your team," Tyler said enthusiastically. "I'm really interested in our subject. I went to Greece twice while I was stationed in Germany with the Army, and that got me hooked on the ancient Greeks and Greek mythology."

"I thought you may be a little older than the rest of us," Sarah said. "How long have you been out of high school?"

"I graduated five years ago and went in the Army, which seemed to be the best thing for me at the time," Tyler replied. "I started here when I got out and am now a sophomore. You folks don't mind having a senior citizen in your group, do you?" he said with an engaging smile.

"Not at all. We have a lot of respect for our elders," I said jokingly.

"Tyler, didn't you say you were from Atlanta?" Rebecca asked.

"Right, I grew up in Atlanta along with my brother and sister who are both older than me. My sister and parents still live here, but my brother doesn't live in Atlanta any more."

"Well, anyway you live in Atlanta, and it's good to have another Atlantan in our group," Sarah said showing some local pride.

"Thanks. I'll try to make a good contribution. Well, I need to go meet someone. I'll see you all later," Tyler said with a broad smile as he got up and left.

"I like him. He has a nice disposition. I wish more people were like that," Rebecca said.

"He does seem very nice," Sarah added. "Also, he's probably more knowledgeable about history than any of the rest of us in the class. That certainly can't hurt us."

## **<u>Six</u>**

It struck me the next morning as I walked to class that being a college freshman in a large city represented a substantial change from my life back home, but I was feeling pretty good about my new circumstances.

Psychology class was boring, but my literature class was interesting. We finished discussing *Agamemnon*. Dr. Chase explained that this play, based on popular ancient Greek myths and legends, was written by Aeschylus in the fifth century B.C. This play and others like it were often written for scheduled competitions. All actors of that period were males, who played both male and female roles. The plays normally had a group of actors in a chorus which provided background narration and insights to complement the dialog and actions of the actors.

*Agamemnon*, like most of the known plays of the ancient Greeks, was considered to be a tragedy. Murders and other terrible acts were normally abundant in these plays. Some of the plays were classified as comedies. Professor Chase explained that Aeschylus, Euripides, and Sophocles were famous writers of tragedies and Aristophanes was noted for comedies.

Rebecca, Sarah and Tyler were already in the student center when I arrived for our two thirty meeting. We discussed various ideas and possibilities and eventually agreed that we would do our presentation on *The Odyssey,* by Homer.

Dr. Chambers' office was located in the History Department on the second floor of Sanderson Hall. The lobby area between the elevators and the entrance to the department contained some glass display cabinets featuring books by faculty members and there were various plaques, pictures and bulletin boards on the walls.

Notices, schedules and other documents about current departmental happenings were found on one of the boards. Another board held colorful flyers and brochures from U.S. and international universities promoting their graduate programs in history. There were also some notices on that board about study abroad programs related to history. The third bulletin board contained employment opportunity listings for individuals with degrees in history. We looked at the items in the lobby briefly before entering the reception area.

A student at the reception desk directed us to Professor Chambers' office. His office was larger than Dr. Wilkens' office, the only other professor's office I had seen so far. It was a little before three o'clock and Dr. Chambers wasn't in his office. I could hear him in some nearby office in a loud conversation with someone. His desk and computer were on the right as you entered his office. There was a table with six chairs in the center of the room. Also, there was a small bookshelf full of books on one wall, but pictures of ancient ruins covered most of the wall space in the office. The pictures were high quality photographs covered with glass in wooden fames.

The pictures really caught your attention upon entering the room and we all started taking a closer look at them. Small engraved brass plaques identified the subject of each photograph. The ruins included the Parthenon and the Erechtheion on the Acropolis in Athens, the Temple of Apollo and the Theatre at Delphi, the Temple of Poseidon at Sounion, the Temple of Hera at Olympia and the Lion's Gate at Mycenae.

Professor Chambers walked in as we were looking at his pictures. He had an agitated look on his face which quickly turned into a smile and he said, "Those pictures are some of my prized possessions. I took those photographs of ancient ruins during my many trips to Greece. I'm sorry I'm a little late for our meeting. Dr. Costanza and I were having one of our stimulating dialogs on the future direction of our department. In the academic world we scholars do have our differences from time-to-time."

"We know you're busy, Dr. Chambers, and appreciate your taking the time to meet with us to discuss our proposed group project," I said.

"I always welcome the chance to get to know my students better, so don't hesitate to see me whenever you'd like," he replied in a manner which affirmed his sincerity. "We don't need to go through introductions since I remember all of your names. What's on your mind?"

"We're interested in doing our project on *The Odyssey*," Sarah said taking charge. "We wonder how you feel about that and would appreciate any advice you might have for us."

"Well, you've already gotten my interest since you have picked one of my favorite books, and one of the most important books ever written," Dr. Chambers replied as he smiled at each of us. "You certainly could base your project on *The Odyssey*. "Have any of you read it?"

"Tyler and I have read it, and that was awhile ago, but we are all interested in reading it or reading it again," Sarah replied.

"Okay. Then we need to discuss just how you would approach your project centered on *The Odyssey*."

"Our assignment would require us to demonstrate how *The Odyssey* has been of importance to Western Civilization over the centuries," Tyler said. "I guess it has influenced authors who have written subsequent books."

"Indeed it has," Dr. Chambers replied. "The story is written as a poem. As best we can determine, Homer was the author, although there has been some speculation that there may have been more than one author. It is believed that the poet Homer, as was the custom of the day, told the story orally, but never reduced it to writing. Some other person probably put it in writing at a later date. It's thought that Homer lived in the eighth century B.C., or as we now often say to be more politically correct, B.C.E., Before the Common Era. In any event, this work has certainly influenced countless writers as well as teachers, artists, intellectuals, historians, etc. over the centuries."

"That may be a lot to cover," Rebecca said.

"That's true. Since your assignment is to give a twenty minute presentation, you may want to limit your scope and discuss how a few prominent writers were influenced by *The Odyssey*."

"Could we do some thinking about this and then give you a more refined proposal before we define the final scope?" Tyler asked.

"Sure. Before you leave, give me a minute to suggest the translation I'd recommend you read. It has some especially helpful footnotes. Also, I'll suggest four other sources which should be of help to you in concluding your project. You may want to divide up some of the reading since this is meant to be a group project."

Professor Chambers neatly wrote some information on a piece of paper and gave it to Sarah. He then said "I know there are many copies of that translation in the book store and the other four books are in the central library. I've also given you some helpful web sites which you should check out."

"Thanks for all of your help, Dr. Chambers," Sarah said with a warm smile.

"It's my pleasure. I've enjoyed our meeting. By the way, I often play pool in the student center on Wednesday evenings. If any of you would ever like to socialize on a more informal basis, stop over there sometime for a game. I find this to be a good way to relax."

"Thanks for the invitation. We may do that," I said. "What time on Wednesdays are you usually there?"

"Normally from about six to nine p.m." he replied as he stood up. "Well, I must get ready for another meeting. I'll see you in class."

We all thanked him and left his office. We paused in the lobby area outside the department and agreed to each get our own copy of *The Odyssey* and finish reading it within the next two weeks. And each of us picked one of the four reference books to review within the same time frame. Rebecca, not surprisingly, wanted to review the web sites. I decided to stay and look at the items in the lobby and the others said goodbye and left.

I read almost everything posted on the three bulletin boards. There were several scheduled departmental functions and lectures and many summaries of accomplishments of faculty members. The glass cabinets contained a book written by Dr. Chambers, *Ancient Greek Architectural Marvels*, and a book by Dr. Costanza, *How Myths and*

*Legends Have Influenced History,* along with books by other faculty members whom I didn't recognize.

By the time I finished looking at the items in the lobby, over an hour had gone by. I left feeling pleased with my plan to major in history.

# **Seven**

I left Sanderson Hall and went to the student center where I bought a copy of the *Atlanta Herald* in order to get an update concerning Dr. Mason's disappearance. The story obviously remained big news since an article on the front page, written by Steve Simmons, was about the case. Dr. Mason was still missing and the search effort and police investigations were still underway. His car, a late model red Corvette, was being analyzed for clues. That had to be the car Tyler told us about. It was found parked in the Woody Gap parking area located where Georgia Highway 60 crosses the Appalachian Trail.

Investigators weren't sure which direction Dr. Mason had gone on the trail and were searching the trail going both directions from the highway.

The Mason's cabin is located about five miles from where his car was found. Mrs. Mason had told investigators she had driven to the parking area about seven thirty p.m. on the evening of his disappearance since she had gotten concerned when he hadn't come home by the expected time of six o'clock. She saw his car and assumed he was still hiking. It was still daylight and the weather was nice. She returned home, assuming Dr. Mason would be home when it got dark.

Mrs. Mason said she had gone back to the cabin where she had some food and wine. She then read while lying on a couch and fell asleep until about six thirty the next morning. When she realized upon waking that Dr. Mason still wasn't home, she really got concerned and drove back to the parking area where she saw his car was still parked in the same place. She then drove back to the cabin and called 911 to report that her husband was missing.

The front page story ended in the middle of the paper and there was a second article by Steve Simmons on that page. He referred to some unnamed sources who had said there was some apparent friction in the marriage of Dr. Mason and his wife Trina. There were also reports of Dr. Mason being seen in restaurants with women other than his wife.

After reading these articles, I began to again think about what could have happened to Dr. Mason. If he really had been running around with other women, could Trina Mason have murdered him or had him murdered in retaliation? If she was involved, maybe she staged a disappearance on the Appalachian Trail, but disposed of his body in some other location. Or, maybe the husband of one of Dr. Mason's lovers, murdered him in some fashion. Or, maybe, Dr. Mason just made it look like he disappeared along the trail. He could have had a car waiting at some other point along the trail and used it to drive to Mexico or California to start a new life.

I reminded myself that I was a college student and not a detective, but still found I was getting increasingly interested in learning what happened to Dr. Mason. As fascinated as I was by this mystery, I knew my school work was piling up. I had to get ready for tomorrow's classes.

The next morning we had an interesting discussion about ancient Egypt in Professor Chambers' class. After class, Rebecca, Sarah and I had lunch on the mall.

As we were sitting down I said, "What did you think about our meeting with Dr. Chambers yesterday?"

Sarah responded, "I'm glad he liked our concept for the project."

"Good meeting," Rebecca added. "I checked out the web sites which he recommended and can see they'll be helpful."

"Weren't the pictures in his office incredible?" Sarah asked.

"Yeah," I replied. "I'd love to see those ruins in person."

"I especially liked the Erechtheion with women statues serving as pillars holding up the roof of one section of the building," Rebecca added. "There was some interesting information about that building on one of the web sites. The women are called Caryatides and there are different theories about what they represent."

"You're really getting into this, girl," Sarah said with a sigh. "I did like the pictures, but Chambers is something else."

"Yeah," Rebecca added. "Not many women would kick him out of bed."

"Cool it, guys," I responded trying to sound frustrated.

"He's hot, but I prefer guys who are a little younger," Rebecca said seductively as she tilted her head toward me and pushed back her hair with her right hand.

I pretended I hadn't noticed Rebecca's gestures, although this was a challenge, and said, "Did you see the articles in last night's Herald about the Dr. Mason case?"

"Yes," Sarah said. "My mom called me after reading it and said her friends can't talk about anything else. They all know Trina Mason and her husband hadn't been on good terms with each other lately since Trina suspected him of having an affair with a nurse from his office."

"I love this inside scoop," Rebecca said. "What about the nurse?"

"Well y'all, her name is Lori Atkins and she's apparently drop-dead gorgeous. But, listen...her husband, Burt, a former officer in the Navy, recently left the service and took a corporate job in Atlanta. While in the Navy, he had been gone most of the time." Sarah said, pausing for breath and then she continued, "Some of my mother's friends are wondering if Burt went after Mason."

"The plot thickens," I said. "What about Trina Mason? Is there any reason to think she may have tried to harm her husband?"

"Well, my mom said Trina was pretty furious. She may have been mad enough to take some action," Sarah replied in a hushed voice.

"There's another interesting angle according to my mom," Sarah added. "Trina had complained to some of her friends that they were having financial problems because of gambling debts run up by Dr. Mason."

"This case would make a good novel," Rebecca said excitedly.

"I was thinking the same thing," Sarah added. "Tomorrow's Saturday. I'll drive us up to where Mason disappeared if you'd like to go. If I could talk you into leaving at eight, we could see some highlights of Atlanta before we head for the mountains."

"It's early, but sounds good to me," Rebecca responded.

"Yeah, we can miss a little beauty sleep and the game's away so we wouldn't miss that," I added. "Seeing things first hand should give me help with my paper."

## **Eight**

The next morning we met at the student center and then walked two blocks to the lot where Sarah's aged, rusty and generously dented black Cadillac was parked.

Once we had gotten into the car, Rebecca said sarcastically, "I love your car, Sarah. What undertaker did you get this from?"

"We'll be riding in luxury today," I added.

"Okay, y'all," Sarah responded in mock frustration. "I get the point."

"Where did you get this beauty?" I asked.

"This is sort of a replacement. Daddy bought me a shiny new convertible a few months ago as a graduation present. It was great while it lasted, but I totaled it in July."

"Awful," Rebecca exclaimed. "I know how you feel. I wiped out my mom's Taurus last year."

"Too bad. In my case, I got this ugly scar as a souvenir," Sarah said as she caressed her left thigh.

"It's the only flaw on your otherwise perfect body," Rebecca said. "It makes you look a little more human."

"It gives you some character," I said, now understanding how she got the scar which I had often wondered about, but had never discussed with her. "So how did you end up with this Caddy?" I asked while patting the dashboard.

"Well, Daddy felt I had to learn a lesson from the experience and said any replacement vehicle would come at my own expense."

"Actually, this old car has some good features," Rebecca said. "The leather seats are still pretty nice."

"It embarrassed me a little at first, but now I love it," Sarah said. "My friends think it's a blast, and I can afford it with my pay from the coroner's office."

"Weather's great today," Rebecca said cheerfully, turning attention away from the car.

"Absolutely," I responded. "What's our game plan Sarah?"

"Since y'all are new to Atlanta, I just want drive around a little while and show you a few highlights. It's pretty interesting. Then, we'll drive up to the mountains and eat somewhere along the way. I expect we'll get back here late afternoon."

"Lead on," I said.

Sarah pulled out of the lot and we were off. Rebecca sat behind Sarah and looked tiny on the spacious seat. Traffic was light most places since it was Saturday morning.

Sarah told us many things about Atlanta as we drove. She was a good guide and the Chamber of Commerce would have been proud of her. We didn't get out of the car, but she stopped in front of certain places of interest. I can't remember everything, but we saw Cyclorama, the Atlanta Zoo, The Fernbank Museum of Natural History, Turner Field, CNN Center, Underground Atlanta, Centennial Olympic Park, and The World of Coca-Cola before we stopped and took a short walk on Peachtree Street.

After our walk, we left the downtown area and Sarah pointed out the Fox Theatre, the Margaret Mitchell House, the Woodruff Arts Center and the Atlanta History Center as we drove north.

"Those are the main sites I wanted you to see in Atlanta today," Sarah said. "We're close to the residential part of Buckhead where I grew up. While I could have commuted to school, my parents and I felt I would benefit from living on campus. That was a no brainer. My mom knew we would be out touring today and asked us to stop in for a quick visit. I haven't been home since classes started. Do you mind?"

"Let's do it," Rebecca said.

"Sure," I added.

"Ryan, look around…awesome!" Rebecca exclaimed as we entered an area with large and impressive homes.

"I've never seen anything like this in Wisconsin," I replied with the same level of awe.

"We're now in a pretty exclusive residential area, I'll have to admit," Sarah said while making a turn.

Every home we passed was very large and stately and they were all on huge exquisitely landscaped lots. The neighborhood was considerably more affluent than any I had ever seen. Judging from Rebecca's comments over the next couple of minutes, I could tell she was as impressed as I was.

"Here we are," Sarah said as she pulled into the long winding driveway leading up to one of the mansions.

When we came to a stop in the circular drive in front of the house I said, "Not too shabby."

"Like, incredible!" Rebecca added excitedly.

"Thanks," Sarah said casually, "come on in."

We walked in after she opened the stylish wooden door with her key. The polished marble floor of the massive open foyer glistened. The oil painting of a fox hunt at the base of the long curved stairway must have been worth a fortune in itself. We went through the great room in back of the foyer, furnished in a safari theme, to the pool area out back where we found Sarah's mother and father reading a newspaper and drinking iced tea.

"Sarah," Mrs. Flemming said warmly as she rose and gave Sarah a hug.

"How's my girl," Sarah's father said as he also rose and gave Sarah a hug. "I know you're not many miles away at Chancellor, but it's seemed like you've been in another world since you started there."

"Sarah, who do we have here?" Mrs. Flemming asked smiling at Rebecca and me.

"Mom and Daddy, this is Rebecca Chan and Ryan Anderson. We're in the same Western civilization class and we've become good friends already."

"It's so nice to meet both of you," Mrs. Flemming said.

Mr. Flemming was still standing and he shook Rebecca's and my hand as he said "Glad you could stop by."

"Sarah said you would be driving up to the mountains," Mrs. Flemming said. "Please have some tea before you go."

"Have a seat," Mr. Flemming said. "My wife and I are both alumni of Chancellor so we can relate to what you're experiencing there as new students. We're glad Sarah decided to follow in our footsteps, even if her brother didn't," he said somewhat jokingly.

"Well, we think it's a great school, y'all, and hope all three of you like it as much as we did," Mrs. Flemming added.

"I'm happy to be there, and like it a lot," Rebecca said. "They certainly have been keeping us very busy though."

"It's a big adjustment for me, but I'm really enjoying it," I said.

We drank our tea and talked about school for about fifteen minutes and then Sarah's mother said, "I understand you may be planning to stop at the point on the Appalachian Trail where Dr. Mason disappeared."

"That's right Mom, and we'll probably look at a few things in Dahlonega while we're up there," Sarah replied. "We've all become interested in Dr. Mason's disappearance and Ryan will be writing a paper about it for one of his classes."

"We've known the Masons for years," Sarah's mother said, "and I'm a friend of Trina Mason. We're so sorry Dr. Mason is missing. This whole matter is tragic."

"We've been looking at the paper this morning," Sarah's dad said, "but there don't seem to be any new leads."

"You all have probably seen references in the press concerning some marital friction and possible affairs," Sarah's mother added. "I shouldn't gossip, but, unfortunately, there is truth in those rumors and that adds to the mystery."

We talked for another few minutes and then Sarah said, getting up from her chair, "We hate to leave, but must get going since we have a lot of driving to do today."

"I guess you're right dear," Sarah's mother said as she also rose. "Are you going to take your friends to Big Canoe while you're in the vicinity?"

"We won't have the time today. Maybe some other time."

"Sarah, it was great seeing you," her dad said as the rest of us stood up. "It was nice meeting you Rebecca and Ryan. Please come see us again," he said as he shook our hands.

"Y'all come back," Sarah's mother added very warmly.

"Thanks for having us," Rebecca said. "I love your home."

"Why, thank you, Rebecca," Sarah's mother replied.

"Nice meeting both of you," I added.

"You are both welcome anytime," Sarah's mother said as she gave Sarah a hug. "Sarah, drive safely and keep in touch."

"Bye Mom," Sarah said and then she hugged her father. "Bye Daddy, I'll see both of you later."

On the way out, I stopped to look at the painting which had caught my eye earlier.

"That used to belong to my granddaddy," Sarah said as she stroked the frame. "It's one of my favorites."

"That was fun," Rebecca said as we drove away. "Your parents are great."

"Yeah, thanks for bringing us, Sarah," I said. "By the way, what's Big Canoe?"

"It's the development where our mountain home is located. Maybe we can get up there sometime. You'd both like it."

## **<u>Nine</u>**

We drove for awhile and ended up on Georgia Highway 400 heading north out of Atlanta. Sarah told us we would take that road to Dahlonega. As we drove along, Sarah explained that the metropolitan area had been expanding northward along Georgia 400 for many years and this highway was the main traffic artery connecting the city with the North Georgia mountains.

"Sarah, this car must be close to thirty years old, but still has a comfortable ride to it," I said.

"It's pretty well-preserved and roomy on the inside but the outside is another story," Rebecca added. "I have room for four more people back here."

"I think its kind of cool," Sarah replied. "You ought to see the look on the faces of some of my friend's parents when I wheel into their circular driveways. They hope nobody's watching and worry that I'll leave oil spots on their precious flagstones."

"That must be priceless," I said with a chuckle. "Actually, the engine sounds good."

"My boyfriend, whom I'm about to dump, is an auto genius and he's done a lot of work on the engine. He even got the air conditioner working."

"Who's this boyfriend?" Rebecca asked.

"We went to school together and he's now here in Atlanta at Georgia Tech. Funny guy. He turned down scholarships at Princeton and Duke since he didn't want to leave home."

"Based on what you said the other day, it sounded like you had some other boyfriends before him," Rebecca said.

"Tell me about it!" Sarah exclaimed. "He's about number five. They've all been fun for awhile, but I seem to eventually get bored with them. Finding a new one has never been a problem."

"Why am I not surprised at that?" Rebecca said trying to sound frustrated, but not succeeding.

"Hey, girl, I doubt you have any trouble finding guys," Sarah said looking in the rearview mirror at Rebecca.

"Not really."

While I was being left out of this female conversation, I didn't mind listening and keeping my mouth shut.

"Are you close to anyone now, Rebecca?" Sarah asked.

"Yes and no. My guy sort of followed me out here. He's a freshman at Georgia in Athens."

"You don't sound too happy about him being around," Sarah said.

"He's okay, but I don't like him as much as I used to. I've only seen him once since we've been in Georgia."

"Ryan, we've been doing all of the talking," Sarah said looking in my direction. "Tell us about your love life."

"Not much to tell."

"You're not very convincing," Rebecca said. "What's your story?"

"Well, I've had the same girlfriend for two years."

"Okay, since you were a jock in high school, was she the gorgeous lead cheerleader who cheered you to victory every game?" Rebecca asked.

"Something like that."

"And what's your honey doing now?" Sarah asked joining in.

"She's going to school in Denver."

"Are you still pretty close?" Rebecca asked.

"I guess so," I replied but, wanting to change the subject I said, "Do you think we'll win the game today?"

My tactic worked. We then talked about football for awhile. I was glad since I wasn't anxious to say any more about Monica.

I looked over at Sarah from time-to-time as we were driving. Despite her privileged upbringing, she was very down-to-earth and probably related well to people from all walks of life. Her personality, somewhat tinged with a "southern belle" element, was very appealing to me. She seemed to treat her beauty casually, but, occasionally, a trace of her underlying elegance would shine through.

I also glanced at Rebecca a few times. She smiled at me playfully and asked me some questions about myself as we drove along. She was not beautiful in the same sense as Sarah, but had a sensuous aura which she skillfully displayed when she saw fit to do so.

"Well, here we are in the central square of Dahlonega," Sarah said, bringing me out of my private thoughts about my traveling companions. "That building on the left is the old Lumpkin County Court House. It's no longer the court house and has been taken over by the Georgia Department of Natural Resources. It's now the Gold Museum," she continued as she pulled into a parking spot. "Come on, let's go in; I want to give you history fans a little North Georgia history lesson as part of our tour today."

"My, this is a quaint town," Rebecca said. "Speaking of history, I love the look of all these buildings around the old court house."

"Yeah, they're really well-preserved. I like to come here," Sarah replied. "I especially like the little bookstore over there and you can get the best home made candy in there," she continued as she pointed to two stores.

"These buildings look like something out of a Norman Rockwell painting," I said as we entered the building.

"You're my guests, and the admission fee is on me," Sarah announced.

Rebecca and I protested a little as Sarah paid the small fee for our tickets. We were greeted and hosted by two pleasant attendants who had Department of Natural Resources patches on their uniform shirts. They gave us a brief commentary on what we would see in the museum and handed each of us a pamphlet. We were just in time to see a movie which was shown on the second floor in the old court room.

The movie was very interesting. We learned how gold was discovered in Dahlonega in the early 1800's and a gold rush took place in the region from about 1818 until 1861. There was so much gold being found that a U.S. Mint operated in Dahlonega for over twenty years. As the precious metal became harder to find in

Dahlonega, it was discovered in California, and large numbers of prospectors fled Dahlonega to take part in the gold rush out West.

While the boom had subsided, many mines continued to operate around Dahlonega. However, by the end of World War Two, most of them had ceased to operate. One commercial mine continues to operate and there are still a few prospectors who look for gold on their own. The movie featured interviews with some citizens who had come from generations of gold miners. They gave some engrossing accounts about how their fathers, grandfathers and other relatives had searched for gold their whole lives, with all of the attendant successes and failures.

Following the movie we saw the old jury room and judge's chambers and then carefully looked at all of the exhibits on both floors of the museum. I was fascinated by everything, especially a room which dealt with the Dahlonega Mint.

When we were finished, we thanked the attendants for their help and walked back toward Sarah's car.

"Sarah, nice history lesson," I said.

"I didn't know gold had been mined around here," Rebecca added. "That was neat."

"Glad you liked it," Sarah said cheerfully. "Now let's have some lunch before we leave."

Sarah took us to a quaint Italian restaurant where we had pizza. As we headed for her car, she led us into the candy shop which she had pointed out earlier. There she bought each of us a chocolate-covered confection with caramel and nuts in the center. These were delicious and I wished I had more than one.

We also spent a few minutes in the small book store Sarah liked. There we saw some books about the Appalachian Trail and many books of local interest.

We drove north out of Dahlonega and got on Georgia Highway 60. We began climbing higher and higher in the mountains. Sarah explained that the Mason's cabin was in the general area, but she wasn't sure exactly where it was located. We had risen to a fairly high elevation after fifteen or twenty minutes and stopped to look down at a vast plain far below. The view was breathtaking.

"What a fabulous view," Rebecca said. "I had no idea you had mountains this high in Georgia."

"Our mountains are not as high as the Rockies, but we're still proud of them," Sarah replied.

## **<u>Ten</u>**

After a short drive we came to the point where the Appalachian Trail crossed the road. There were parking areas on both sides of the highway and we pulled into the one on our right. There were many vehicles in the lots, including two sheriff cars in each lot. There were signs and displays in both areas. A sign told us we were at Woody Gap. After getting out of the car we noticed a rock on the ground labeled "Appalachian Trail." It had an arrow which pointed left to "Springer Mountain" and an arrow pointing right which said, "Maine." From my earlier research, I remembered that the trail began at Springer Mountain.

"Judging from all of these cars, I imagine that search parties are still looking for Dr. Mason," Sarah said.

We walked over to a sign which said there was a two dollar parking fee and envelopes were provided for that purpose. Sarah took out one of the envelopes.

"According to one of the news reports, Mason filled one of these out on the day of his disappearance," Sarah said as she passed the envelope to Rebecca and me.

I studied the envelope and saw it was provided by the Southern Region USDA Forest Service. There was a detachable flap designed to be hung from a vehicle's rear view mirror. The flap had a number which corresponded with the number on the envelope. Money was to be placed in the envelope and envelopes were to be put in a green box.

Sarah put two dollars in the envelope and followed the procedure.

Sarah then said. "They said in the paper that Mason's Corvette was found in this parking lot, but the envelope containing his payment was found in the box over in that lot," she said while pointing across the highway.

"I wonder which way he went on the trail," I said.

"They don't know, and that's why the search parties are looking in both directions," Sarah responded. "Why don't we walk on this side going toward Maine for awhile and then we can cross over the highway and walk in the direction of Springer Mountain."

"Let's do it," Rebecca said.

We left the parking area and started down the trail. We saw a sign which said it was 2.9 miles to Miller Gap.

"What are those white marks on the trees?" Rebecca asked.

"Ryan can probably answer that," Sarah replied.

"They're called blazes," I said. "They show you where the trail goes if it isn't obvious. In the early days, people used hatchets to make white marks by removing bark from the trees and that's where that name trailblazers comes from. Now days the marks are made with paint by volunteer groups who maintain this and other trails."

"That's smart," Rebecca responded. "So far it's been pretty easy walking."

"I haven't walked the trail from this entry point, but I've been on other parts of it in Georgia," Sarah said. "It can get quite rigorous, or maybe even a little dangerous, in some sections if you lose your footing."

"It's so peaceful and beautiful here, it's hard to imagine someone getting lost or attacked along the trail," Rebecca said.

"That's right," I added, "It really makes you wonder what happened to Dr. Mason if, in fact, he even was on the trail when he disappeared."

"Maybe nothing happened to him and he is on his way up to Maine," Sarah said with a grin.

"Maybe so," I said, "Or, perhaps he hiked up the trail several miles, got picked up by a girlfriend, and is now starting a new life in Costa Rica."

"Aren't you two creative," Rebecca kidded. "Maybe Burt Atkins learned of the alleged affair, killed Dr. Mason along the trail, hauled his body away and dumped it in a North Carolina lake sufficiently weighted down so it will never be discovered."

We continued speculating about what might have happened to Dr. Mason and also talked about more carefree subjects as we walked along. The trail was much like I expected it would be and I enjoyed experiencing it first hand after reading about it for so long.

Rebecca walked with ease. Sarah kept pace with us, but seemed to have some stiffness in her left leg from time-to-time. They were wearing shorts. I tried not being so obvious, but my eyes kept scanning their smooth and shapely legs as they negotiated the trail.

The sounds of the birds singing and the squirrels in the trees were soothing. There was a faint smell of pine and I caught an occasional fragrance from the wild flowers we passed. It was peaceful and I felt very relaxed. We walked for what must have been thirty minutes and didn't see any other people along the way.

"I haven't seen anything that looks suspicious," Rebecca said after we had been walking in silence for a few minutes.

"If there were any clues, the search parties may have already found them," I said.

"You would think so," Sarah said. "Are you ready to turn around?"

We agreed. The walk back was uneventful. As on our outbound leg, we saw no people on the return trip.

We got back to the parking lot and Sarah gave us some bottled water from her trunk.

"Thanks, I needed that," Rebecca said appreciatively.

"What, no beer?" I said.

"Sorry, dear. That's all I have along today."

We then walked across the highway to the other parking lot. A young couple and their two small children were looking at the main sign in the parking area. We saw no other people.

As we left the parking area and got on the trail, we saw a sign which informed us that Springer Mountain was 20.02 miles ahead.

After walking a few minutes, it was obvious the contour of the land was much steeper than it had been on the other side of the highway. The terrain to our right sloped upward and the terrain to the left of the trail sloped steeply down hill.

"Look how much it drops off in that direction," Rebecca said. "What if Dr. Mason was shot and fell down there? A body could roll down a long way if it didn't get hung up in the trees and bushes."

I didn't respond since I started hearing voices coming in our direction and soon saw what I assumed was a search party approaching us. We then met a group of six men, led by two people in sheriff's uniforms. They were talking excitedly but stopped talking as we met them. A couple of them nodded at us and said hello as they went by, but they seemed to be in a hurry with no desire to talk to us. One of the officers was carrying a small cardboard box with the top flaps closed.

"They must be working on the Mason case," Rebecca said. "I wonder what was in that box."

We stopped walking and I said, "They probably were one of the search parties all right. They seemed to be pretty excited."

Sarah said. "Why don't we wait a couple of minutes and follow them to see what we can find out?"

Rebecca and I agreed and we soon headed back to the parking lot.

As we approached the parking area, we saw the men gathered near the two sheriff's cars. Their backs were toward us and most of them were standing near the cardboard box which was sitting on the hood of one of the cars. The flaps of the box were folded open. Based on their animated discussion and gestures, the contents of the box must have been important.

Rebecca led the way over to the sign where the parking fee envelopes were stored and she said quietly, "Let's each take one of these envelopes and pretend to be reading them standing near enough to hear what they're saying without being too obvious. Then, we can try to see what's in the box. They may keep talking if we don't seem to be paying attention to them."

We then followed Rebecca to the side of a car within earshot of the men and formed a small circle facing each other as we looked at our envelopes.

"Billy old Buddy, I told you three times, they wasan't there last night when we quit at dark," one officer said to the other officer.

"Then, somebody must'a put 'em out there last night or early this mor'nin," Billy replied as he looked at the first officer. "They weren't too obvious, Frank. Could ya have missed 'em yesterday or before that?"

"We was lookin' so close, we would never'a missed 'em. I know the candles is small, but we wouldn'da missed 'em before."

"Were they burnin' when ya found 'em?"

"No, but some had been burnin' longer'en others."

"Are you sure they were a hundred feet apart?" Billy asked Frank impatiently.

"Yeah, boy! We paced off all the spaces between 'em."

"Okay, and, it was about a thirty minute walk from this parking lot to the first candle, right?"

"Right, dependin' on how fast ya walk."

"Sure. Well, that's all we can do here. Let's take what we got back to the office."

Sensing what was about to happen, the three of us quietly walked by the open box and looked inside without calling too much attention to ourselves. We kept on walking across the highway and got into Sarah's car.

Sarah started the engine to get the air conditioner running and said, "It looked like there were about ten small candles in the box. Is that what you saw?"

"Yeah," Rebecca said. "They were white and maybe about six inches long."

"Do you think the candles have anything to do with the Mason case?" I asked.

"The sheriffs or deputies, or whatever they were, must have thought so, based on what we heard them discussing," Rebecca replied.

"The candles certainly may relate to the case," Sarah said. "If someone harmed or kidnapped the doctor, perhaps that person left the candles as some form of trademark or sadistic clue as killers sometimes do in the movies."

"Yeah," Rebecca said. "Why else would someone come out here and put ten candles along the trail spaced one hundred feet apart?"

"Maybe the candles have nothing to do with the Mason case," I said. "But, I don't know why else someone would have put them out along the trail, especially now when there is so much publicity surrounding the case."

"Do you think the investigators will tell the press about the candles?" Sarah asked.

"They may want to keep it quiet if they think it would help them pin a crime on someone," I responded. "If there had been no public disclosure about the candles and they found someone who knew about them, that person could be a prime suspect."

"Or, they may tell the public about the candles hoping that may cause someone to identify the guilty party," Rebecca said.

"Are you both as fascinated by this case as I am?" Sarah asked excitedly. "You sound like it."

"Absolutely," Rebecca replied.

"Same here," I added. "It's getting even more interesting."

We drove back through Dahlonega where Sarah showed us North Georgia College and the Smith House, a popular restaurant known for its family style meals. We had learned earlier at the Gold Museum that the U.S. Mint building had been donated to the college in 1871 about ten years after it had been closed. The building later burned down, but the college's current administration building stands on the foundation of the old mint building. The roof on the tower of the building, which is covered in thin gold leaf, glistened in the afternoon sun as we drove by.

Mike was gone when I got back to my room. I had some food from my small refrigerator and decided to not go out and look for a party after I didn't find anyone around in my hall. I felt a little weird being home on a Saturday night, but was tired and it really didn't bother me too much. I watched some TV, read for awhile and went to bed about midnight.

While I was physically tired, my mind was active and I couldn't fall asleep. I found myself thinking about the candles we had seen in the box. Did they have anything to do with the disappearance of Dr. Mason? Why else would the candles have been placed along the trail by someone? The candles must be some kind of clue related to the Mason case; it seemed to me that was the only logical explanation. If my assumption was correct, what was the significance of the candles?

Why would ten candles be placed along the trail one hundred feet apart? Whoever put them there had some kind of plan if he or she took the time to place them in that fashion. Was the number ten significant? Was the distance of one hundred feet significant? Were the candles calling attention to that stretch of the trail for some reason? Was Dr. Mason's body in that area somewhere? Did the candles symbolize something else? Maybe that was it, but, if so, what did they symbolize? They apparently had been lit when they were put in place by an unknown person. If so, there would have been a row of lights or a row of fires. That reminded me of something, but what was it?

Then it struck me. The candles reminded me of Agamemnon.

# **Eleven**

The next morning I went to the student center to wait for Rebecca and Sarah. Sarah was taking us to see *Gone With the Wind* at CNN Center. There was a copy of the Sunday *Atlanta Herald* in the lounge area which had a story by Steve Simmons on the front page. The headline read "Possible Clue in Mason Case." I was surprised the candles had become public knowledge so fast, but the article explained how investigators had found candles along the Appalachian Trail and they were considered potentially related to the Mason case. Simmons reported, as we already knew, that ten white candles were found along the trail, west of the Woody Gap parking area. The candles were said to have been partially burned and were spaced one hundred feet apart.

It was decided to make the finding of the candles known to the general public in case this may prompt someone to come forward with information helpful in solving the case. Simmons ended the article by saying the candles had been sent to the state crime lab for analysis and authorities were now doing a concentrated search of the area surrounding the trail where the candles were found.

As I finished reading the article, both Sarah and Rebecca arrived. They hadn't seen the article and read it while we sat there.

"Amazing," Rebecca said. "I'm surprised the investigators made the candles public."

"Me too," I said.

"I feel like we are really drawn into this case now, having seen what we did yesterday," Sarah said.

"Yeah," I responded. "I've got to tell you something. I had a strange thought about it as I was trying to get to sleep last night. It was pretty far-fetched."

"What was that, Ryan?" Rebecca asked.

"It probably doesn't mean anything, but, we recently read *Agamemnon* in my literature class. In that play, fires were lit along the route from Troy to Argos to signal that Agamemnon was returning home to Argos at the end of the Trojan War. This forewarned his wife, Clytemnestra, and her lover, Aegistus, and they killed Agamemnon in his house when he got back home. The candles along the Appalachian Trail reminded me of that trail of fires."

"Interesting," Sarah said. "Do you think Trina Mason got fed up enough with her husband to kill him like Clytemnestra killed Agamemnon?"

"Maybe," I replied.

"Scorned women have found all kinds of ways of doing away with their husbands," Rebecca said. "Maybe she did do something to get even with him for cheating on her."

The movie was long, but I was glad to see it since I hadn't seen it before. While I wasn't sure how accurate it was, it certainly presented a vivid picture of life in the aristocratic South at the time of the Civil War.

While Rhett Butler had his faults, I found him to be a likable character. I also enjoyed Scarlett. She was a real conniver, but I had to admire her resilience and survival instinct.

As we drove back to campus, I realized there were some things about Sarah which reminded me of Scarlett, especially her self-confidence and some of her facial expressions.

In future weeks there were a few occasions when Sarah seemed to mimic Scarlett when she was trying to be particularly persuasive or alluring. That always intrigued me when I saw it happen, but I never said anything about it to Sarah.

Mike and I went to the student center and had something to eat after I got back from the movie. He was familiar with the Mason case and had read the morning article about the candles in the *Atlanta Herald*. I explained to Mike about the trip which Sarah, Rebecca and

I had made to the Appalachian Trail and how we had seen the candles found by the searchers.

After we had finished eating, we shot baskets with some other guys for awhile on an outdoor court near the dorm. It felt good to get the exercise. After that, Mike stayed at the dorm and I went to the library. I started reading *The Odyssey* and quickly became interested in the story which began with the goddess Athena telling her father Zeus, the king of the gods, that it was time to free Odysseus from Calypso's spell. Through this spell, she had kept Odysseus as her lover on her island for many years preventing his return to his home in Ithaca following the Trojan War.

During the lengthy period which followed Odysseus's departure for Troy, his wife Penelope had remained loyal to him, but numerous suitors became increasingly troublesome as they consumed Odysseus's food and wine and courted Penelope on the assumption Odysseus would never return.

Zeus was supportive and Athena helped release Odysseus from Calypso. Odysseus then resumed his journey back to his wife and his son Telemachus.

I became engrossed and read for over an hour before I stopped to write a short paper for English.

During the first part of Dr. Chambers' class the next morning, he finished discussing ancient Egypt. He then began talking about the importance of the ancient Greeks in the foundations of our Western civilization. We would first cover the earliest phases of the Greek civilization, and would end talking about Alexander the Great and the Hellenistic period which followed his death. However, most of our discussion would focus on the Classical period when the greatest cultural breakthroughs took place.

Following that introduction, we spent the rest of the class discussing how religion, myths, and legends impacted all aspects of Greek culture.

After class, Rebecca, Sarah and I went to the student center to get some lunch. As we walked by the large-screen TV, we noticed that a reporter from one of the local stations was talking about the Mason case so we sat down to see what we could learn. The reporter announced that the lead investigator, Richard Webb, was about to hold a press conference. Mr. Webb read a prepared statement in which he said Dr. Mason had not yet been found, but they were aggressively following up on all leads and interviewing many witnesses. He mentioned that they were piecing information together and were hopeful of solving the case soon. He then said he would try to answer a few questions.

A tall woman in a red dress asked, "Do you feel Dr. Mason came to some foul play along the Appalachian Trail?"

"We feel that is most likely what happened, but there may be some other reason for his disappearance."

Steve Simmons was present and he asked, "Do you think Dr. Mason could be either dead or alive?"

"He could be either based on what we know at this point."

A familiar reporter from one of the local TV stations asked, "Assuming Dr. Mason was killed or kidnapped, do you have any suspects?"

"There is no evidence of a crime at this point and, therefore, there is nothing to have suspects for."

An older woman with a cane asked, "Can you comment on the candles found along the trail?"

"We're not sure of their significance," Mr. Webb answered. "However, they are being carefully analyzed and search efforts are being intensified near where they were found."

A distinguished older man in a blue suit asked, "There seems to be some fairly strong evidence that there was friction in the Mason's marriage due to an affair the doctor was having with Lori Atkins, a nurse from his office. Can you comment on that?"

"No comment at this time."

Steve Simmons then bluntly asked, "Could Burt Atkins, Mrs. Atkins husband who recently returned from the Navy, have any involvement with this case?"

"He's one of the people we have been questioning." Mr. Webb replied.

"Have you learned anything helpful from Dr. Mason's wife?" Steve Simmons blurted out over other reporters who were trying to ask questions.

"We have, obviously, had various conversations with Mrs. Mason and she has been cooperating in the investigation."

A young woman in a white dress asked, "There have been news reports indicating Dr. Mason may have had some financial problems due to gambling debts. Can you comment on that?"

"There is some truth in that," Mr. Webb said. "I'll take only one more question."

The distinguished man in the blue suit asked, "Is it possible, due to gambling debts or his affair, that Dr. Mason voluntarily disappeared to get away from his problems?"

"We haven't ruled out that possibility, but feel it is more likely his disappearance was not voluntary. Thanks for coming ladies and gentlemen."

A commercial then replaced Mr. Webb on the screen.

We then got some food and went to the mall to eat. Once we were seated on the grass, Rebecca said. "It didn't take long for some of the rumors about Dr. Mason to become very public."

"These things were not secrets, so I'm not surprised," Sarah responded. "Hey y'all, I picked up a little more gossip last night in talking with my mom. She and her friends are still caught up in this case. Burt Atkins, while he was in the Navy, spent a lot of time in Greece and the Mediterranean before he returned to Atlanta."

"So?" Rebecca asked.

"So," Sarah responded, "if there is any substance to Ryan's theory about a relationship between Mason's disappearance and Agamemnon, maybe Burt knows something about that ancient story."

"Interesting," I said. "Maybe it means something. He certainly had a motive for foul play if that's what happened to Mason."

"Would your coroner's office get involved if Dr. Mason turns up dead?" Rebecca asked.

"It would depend on where the body was found," Sarah responded. "We'll see what happens."

# **<u>Twelve</u>**

That afternoon, I sat down in U.S. history behind Rebecca just as Dr. Costanza was beginning to speak. Rebecca smiled at me and quietly greeted me as I passed her.

I noticed Dr. Costanza had written the names of many American Indian tribes on the white board in front of the room. To the right of those names, he had written "Myths and Legends." He began talking about how tribes had been formed and how they differed from each other. I was trying to concentrate, but my mind began to wander.

Rebecca had her silky black hair in a pony tail tied with a ribbon which matched her sleeveless pale green shirt. This left part of her neck visible and I could see she was wearing a thin beaded leather necklace which rested lightly on her flawless skin.

After we had been sitting for awhile, Rebecca clasped her hands behind her neck and held them in that position for a few seconds while she flexed her arms slightly and stretched her shoulder muscles. She worked out a lot, and I wondered if this was an exercise which she did to keep limber or maybe the gesture was meant to get my attention. Her hands were perfectly formed. She wore a sports watch on her left wrist and had two gold rings on her right hand.

Rebecca unclasped her hands and turned her head to the left when the student next to her dropped his pencil on the floor. She watched while he bent down to pick it up. Rebecca seemed to know I was looking at her and she turned back and smiled at me before turning to face the front of the room.

I found myself comparing Rebecca with Monica Rogers, my girlfriend from high school who was attending college in Colorado. They were both quite attractive, but attractive in much different ways. Monica had the wholesome look of the girl next door. Rebecca, on the other hand, was more exotic and playful.

My mind got back in focus when I heard Dr. Costanza say, "I'd now like to spend the rest of today's session discussing the myths, and legends of the tribes which we just talked about. There are many parallels between some of their beliefs and those found in other ancient civilizations. I'll use Greece as an example since it offers some of the best comparisons. Let me write a few things on the board."

Dr. Costanza then wrote these words on the board: "Agamemnon," "Prometheus," "Odysseus," "Sisyphus," "Tantalus," and "Pandora."

"Most of you probably recognize some of these names," he said in a challenging fashion. "Those of you who are particularly well informed could tell us a little story about all of them."

I felt reasonably competent since I had heard of Pandora and had recently read some about Agamemnon and Odysseus. Also, I was about to learn about Prometheus. However, I was not familiar with Sisyphus and Tantalus.

We then discussed the six names. Most of the students knew about as much as I did, but it was obvious that three students had a good knowledge of all of the names. Dr. Costanza skillfully steered the discussion and I was glad to learn about Sisyphus and Tantalus.

Sisyphus, after angering Zeus and tricking Pluto, was punished by being sent to Tartarus, the part of The Underworld reserved for evil people. There, Sisyphus was forced to roll a heavy boulder up a steep hill throughout eternity. He could never complete his task, since each time he was able to get the boulder near the top of the hill, it would roll back down again.

Tantalus tried to trick the gods by feeding them pieces of his son, whom he had butchered, to see if the gods would be able to notice that they were eating human flesh. They were not fooled. As his punishment he was also sent to Tartarus where he was eternally tortured by having water and fruit slip away from him each time he tried to drink or eat. His unbearable thirst and appetite were never satisfied. That's where the word tantalize comes from.

After we had talked about the Greek names, Dr. Costanza drew parallels between them and various Indian myths and legends. The similarities fascinated me.

When class was over, I said to Rebecca, "Costanza was on a roll today. That was interesting. Hearing about Tantalus suddenly made me thirsty. Can I buy you a drink?"

"Why Ryan, are you asking me out on a date?" she asked seductively. "That's sweet of you. I'd love some juice."

I smiled and said, "We could call it a date, I guess."

I bought apple juice for each of us and we found a shady place to sit on the grass.

We sat cross-legged facing each other and I said, "Rebecca, you look great today."

Rebecca smiled warmly and said, "Thanks. I was hoping you would notice my outfit today. It's one of my favorites."

She then tilted her head a little and, with a slight frown, said. "I wore it once before, but you didn't say anything to me then."

"I'm sorry about that. I guess I wasn't concentrating that day."

"I guess I'll forgive you. Oh, I got an e-mail last night from my grandfather asking me how school was going," Rebecca said changing the subject. "It was nice hearing from him."

"Where does he live?"

"He and my grandmother live in the Los Angeles area. They were both born in Shanghai, but came to the U.S. as young children with their parents. They're my dad's parents. My mom's parents came to the U.S. from Hong Kong when they were young, but they are no longer alive. They also lived in the Los Angeles area."

"I'm sorry they're no longer living. Since all of your grandparents lived in Los Angeles, is that where your mom and dad were born?"

"Right. They grew up there and met when they were both students at U.C.L.A."

"I guess all of that explains why you don't have a Chinese accent."

"That explains it," Rebecca smiled. "Say, I need some clarification. I heard someone talk about Midwestern values the other day. What does that mean?"

"It may mean different things to different people. To me, it means things like honesty, a good work ethic, friendliness, and following the Golden Rule."

"I like the sound of that. You seem to have Midwestern values, Ryan."

"Thanks."

"We need more of that kind of thinking in the world. It would eliminate many of the problems."

"You're right there. You talked about your grandparents. What about your parents? You said earlier they were divorced."

"Yeah. It happened when my dad fell in love with someone else. It was tough on me at the time, but I'm okay with it now."

"Sorry to hear about that. Did you live with your mother after that?"

"Yeah, it hurt her at first, but she's strong and resourceful and bounced back pretty fast. I've learned a lot from her."

"How about your dad?"

"He's fundamentally a decent person. We still get along fine, but don't see much of each other."

"Was it hard going through high school without your dad around?"

"Well, money was tight and I always worked a lot. But, Mom and I did fine, even though I know I caused her some typical teenage-based anxiety from time-to-time."

"Were you a little wild?"

"Maybe a little," Rebecca announced with a sly smile. "How about you?"

"Oh, probably nothing out of the ordinary. We always had a good time, but, luckily, I didn't get caught for some of the things which could have gotten me in trouble."

"That's comforting. So, what about your parents? You said your dad's a businessman and your mom's an architect."

"Yeah. They're good parents. We get along well most of the time, but, like you, I know I've stirred up a little anxiety once in awhile. I've, however, learned a lot from both of them."

"Like what?"

"I've learned some things about being practical from my dad and my mom has maybe given me an interest in looking for details."

"What do you mean by that?"

"When you go into a room, meet a new person or walk through the woods with her, she always notices and talks about interesting details like facial features, colors, smells, feelings, form and substance, and things like that. It's really amazing how much she gets out of a simple situation."

"Interesting."

"Yeah, and I've picked some of that from her. My mind wanders now and then and I find myself thinking about things like that."

"I'm intrigued. It's nice to hear about your artistic side. You might make a good poet or writer someday."

"Maybe, but probably not likely. Hey, what did you think about Costanza's class today?"

"He really got into it and even acted half-way human. Actually, he made some interesting points."

"Yeah," I replied. "When he was talking about Agamemnon, I was surprised how he focused on the trail of fires. For some strange reason, I almost expected he would relate them to the candles on the Appalachian Trail."

"He did act a little strange about that, now that you mention it."

We relaxed and talked for several more minutes until Rebecca said she needed to go work out.

As we stood up, my eyes surveyed her body. She was solidly built but still very feminine. Her legs were like those of a world class figure skater, strong, yet well proportioned.

"Rebecca, all of your working out is really serving you well."

She followed my eyes with a knowing smile, opened her mouth to say something, changed her mind, tilted her head to the side while still looking at me, and smiled again.

She then slowly pulled on her backpack while holding me in her gaze and said, "Thanks for the drink," as she turned slowly and walked away, giving me one glance over her shoulder after she had gone a few feet.

I just stood there and watched her until she left my line of sight. It was like I was falling under her spell and I briefly imagined how

Odysseus must have felt on Calypso's island. I regained my composure after a few moments and went back to my room.

I listened to a couple of messages on my answering machine and then called Steve Simmons. Fortunately he picked up the phone on the second ring. I was glad he was in. I told him I had seen him on TV at the morning press conference and he seemed pleased I'd watched the telecast. Steve said he felt there must have been some type of breakthrough in the case, but he didn't know for sure what was going on. His contacts were excited about something, but they weren't returning his phone calls. He was working hard to learn what was happening and urged me to closely monitor the Herald and other news sources for a possible significant development in the Mason case. He was in a hurry, so we didn't talk long.

Mike and one of his friends from the crew team came in and we talked about some girls they had met at their last regatta. The more we talked, the more I realized they were making up all or most of their story. The more I said I didn't believe them, the wilder their tale became. We all had a good laugh and then shot some baskets and got something to eat.

About nine, I went to the library. I started reading *Prometheus Bound* since we were going to cover it in literature class in the morning.

My mind wandered to Rebecca. I closed my eyes and could see her sitting across from me on the grass. She was smiling at me as she talked and was looking deeply into my eyes. I then visualized the back of her head as I had sat behind her in class and saw her turn and smile at me when the student dropped his pencil.

Then, I thought of Monica. We had known each other since grade school and had become inseparable our last two years of high school. We were very close and had talked of possibly getting married after college. Yet, we knew that four years of separation could affect our relationship. We had been staying in touch via e-mail and had two phone conversations since we went off to school. I missed her and I knew she missed me. It was hard being separated and I looked forward to seeing her over the Christmas holidays.

While I was becoming increasingly attracted to Rebecca, I wanted to remain loyal to Monica. I was bothered by this dilemma, but eventually put both of them out of my mind and was able to concentrate on the play and finish reading it.

I liked it almost as much as *Agamemnon*, and could appreciate why these works by Aeschylus had remained so popular for over two thousand years. "Tragedy" was the right label for both of them.

Agamemnon certainly came to a tragic death. While Prometheus didn't die since he was an immortal, he suffered almost unbearably. Prometheus had offended Zeus and he was punished by being bound to a rock where an eagle tore out his liver every day. The process continued since his liver was restored each time it was devoured.

Next, I picked up *The Odyssey*. I read about Odysseus' son Telemachus and how he had gone out in search of his father. I also read how Odysseus survived a very treacherous voyage at sea after leaving Calypso's island before he landed on Skheria Island where he was befriended by Alkinoos who ruled that land. After building up a level of trust, Odysseus began telling Alkinoos and his followers of the adventures he and his men had endured while attempting to return to their homes following the Trojan War.

I had a message from Laurel Masters on my answering machine when I got back to my room. She asked me to call as soon as I got the message. I called and she wanted to talk about the idea of forming a band as we had discussed earlier. She and some of her friends from the music school wanted to meet with me. It was midnight, but no one was ready for bed so we met in the student center twenty minutes later.

It worked out great. Laurel introduced me to Adam Walsh, Bob Martin and Sergio Ortiz. They were all in a music theory class with her and shared my idea of forming a band.

Adam was a drummer and was from Louisville. Bob was a trumpet student from Seattle, but had played bass in a group in high school. Sergio was from Madrid and loved to sing. He wanted to be lead singer and play rhythm guitar. He was very animated and personable. He gave us a sample of his vocal talents and we knew he was right for the job.

Laurel was the obvious choice for keyboard and that left me as the lead guitarist.

We seemed to get along well and set up a time to practice the next day. Laurel agreed to find a practice room.

## **Thirteen**

Since Steve Simmons had urged me to be alert for developments in the Mason case, the next morning I got up early and watched the local news before getting ready for class. Mike had left very early for crew practice.

Following a commercial, the anchorwoman announced that there was a surprising development in the Mason case. Yesterday afternoon, his body had been found near the Appalachian Trail west of the Woody Gap parking area. Searchers had found the body while focusing their search in the area where the candles had been found. In that area, the terrain falls off sharply on the south side of the trail. The body was found about two hundred feet below the trail in a gully and was not readily visible since it was nearly covered with branches and leaves.

Authorities did not announce the discovery until this morning when they confirmed the body to be that of Dr. Mason. It appeared he had been murdered, but formal findings would not be released until forensic experts conducted an examination. The body was found wrapped in a large velvet robe and there was a knife inside the robe next to Dr. Mason's body. The preliminary conclusion was that he had been killed with that knife by some unknown person or persons who had tried to hide the body near the scene of the crime. The reporter ended the story by saying that no more information had been released, but an update would be given, by the lead investigator, Richard Webb, at three o'clock in the afternoon.

I turned off the television and reflected in amazement on what I had just heard.  First candles were found, and now Dr. Mason had been found dead, wrapped in a robe with a knife.  A trail of fires had forewarned Clytemnestra and Aegistus that Agamemnon was coming home and they killed him with a knife after entangling him in robes.  While it was hard to believe, it seemed that Mason's killer was trying to replicate the killing of Agamemnon.

I had trouble paying attention in my psychology class since I kept thinking about Peter Mason.

I closed my eyes and could visualize the portion of the trail which Rebecca, Sarah and I had seen to the west of the Woody Gap parking area.  The murder had taken place further down the trail from where we had walked, but, I assumed the terrain was similar to the region we had seen where the ground to the south of the trail dropped sharply down hill away from the trail.  If the murderer killed or knocked Dr. Mason unconscious on the trail, it would have been easy for him to roll the body down the steep bank a good distance below the trail by manipulating it around trees and bushes.

Investigators should be able to determine if he was, indeed, stabbed with the knife.  Maybe they would find clues concerning how many people were involved from footprints or other clues.  Maybe the knife could be traced and maybe it would have fingerprints.

The big question, was, who was responsible for the murder?  Was the doctor killed by one person or more than one?  Possible suspects could include Burt Atkins, Trina Mason, Lori Atkins, or a criminal who may have financed the doctor's gambling debts.  Maybe more clues would come out of the afternoon news conference.

Professor Chase opened our world literature class by asking if any of us had heard the morning news reports about the discovery of Dr. Mason's body.  Many of us had, and for the benefit of the other students, she summarized what had been reported on TV.  She then asked if we saw any relationship between the murder and anything we had studied in our class.  I was about to respond when another student excitedly commented on the similarities between the Mason case and *Agamemnon.*

"That's right," Dr. Chase said.  "The candles found along the trail are similar to the beacons between Troy and Argos and the robe and knife found with Dr. Mason remind us of us how Agamemnon was killed. Maybe it's just coincidence, but there do seem to be some striking similarities between the two murders."

"Do you think this means the murderer knew about the story of Agamemnon?" I asked.

"It's certainly possible," Dr. Chase answered. "The story of Agamemnon's death is a well known Greek legend. While we learned about it through Aeschylus's play, most people who know anything about Greek mythology would know about Agamemnon."

"*Agamemnon* was presented at a local theatre in Atlanta last year, and that could have acquainted many people with the story, who were unfamiliar with it," a student volunteered.

"Well, as interesting as all of this may be, we must focus on our class material," Dr. Chase said. "Let's talk about *Prometheus Bound*."

At the end of the period, Dr. Chase said, "I hope you've found our readings thus far to have been stimulating. Our next work, as you know, is Dante's *Divine Comedy*. While this was written in the early thirteen hundreds, you'll find that Dante makes references to many ancient Greek figures. It's in three parts: *Inferno, Purgatory,* and *Paradise*." It's a fairly long work and therefore we'll only cover the first two parts. I'll give you a recap of *Paradise*, but you will not be tested on that. Please read the assigned pages of *Inferno* for our next class."

It was warm and sunny, but not as humid as in recent days. That was a relief. I didn't see anyone I knew in the student center to eat with, so I had my lunch on a bench in the shade by the mall. After eating, I pulled *The Odyssey* out of my backpack and read about how Odysseus and his men had been through many adventures before all of his men were lost and Odysseus ended up alone on Calypso's island where she kept him under her spell for seven years.

Initially, the warriors had battled the Cyclones, been tempted by the Lotus Eaters, and had a frightening ordeal with the fierce one-eyed Cyclops. These adventures were followed by the storms unleashed when Odysseus' men foolishly opened the bag containing the winds of Aiolos and by their disastrous encounter with the Laistrygonians before Odysseus and his small band of survivors landed on the Island of Circe.

Their encounter with Circe was fascinating. She was a beautiful goddess who initially turned some of Odysseus' men into swine. With help from Hermes, Odysseus was able to convince Circe to turn his companions back to men. Circe and her maids and nymphs then became very kind to Odysseus and his men and provided them with an idyllic environment of food, wine and companionship for many months. Eventually, when Odysseus and his men wanted to leave to continue their journey home, Circe said that they would be required to consult with the seer Teiresias in the Underworld before they could reach their homeland.

While I hated to stop reading, it was almost three o'clock so I left the bench and went back to my dorm room to watch the news update on the Mason case.

Mike was not there and I turned on the television just as the report began. The lead investigator, Richard Webb, who had given the earlier press conference, first read a prepared statement. He indicated that the search workers had been concentrating their efforts along the portion of the trail where the candles had been found, looking several hundred feet on both sides of the trail. The area was densely wooded and the terrain was very steep, making the search process difficult. The body was located so far from the trail and it was so well hidden, it had not previously been found. Dr. Mason had been stabbed multiple times and his body had been wrapped in a large purple velvet bath robe along with the knife which had apparently been used to kill him. An autopsy would soon be performed and investigators were carefully reviewing the crime scene and exploring other leads.

"I'll now take a few questions," Mr. Webb said after he had finished his statement.

"Do you have any suspects in the murder?" Steve Simmons asked.

"We have no formal suspects at this time, but we are continuing to speak with many people who may be able to provide useful information," Mr. Webb replied.

"Is the doctor's wife a suspect?" a familiar female TV reporter asked.

"She has been cooperating in our investigation and is not a formal suspect at this time," Mr. Webb answered.

A tall man in a blue sport coat said, "It appears Dr. Mason had been having an affair with Lori Atkins, his office nurse. Is her husband, Burt Atkins, a suspect?"

"Not at this time, but we hope to have more conversations with him," Mr. Webb replied.

"Is their any explanation concerning why the doctor's body was wrapped in a robe?" a middle-age woman in a beige pants suit asked.

"We have no explanation at this point, but obviously we are looking for one. Also, we will be trying to determine where the robe came from."

A gray haired woman said, "I'm assuming that the body had decomposed, at least to some extent. If so, could you be sure he was stabbed?"

"We feel confident about that due to the slits in the robe and his clothing. It appears he was trapped under the robe and stabbed multiple times.'

The gray haired woman followed with, "Is there any possibility Dr. Mason faked a murder and killed himself?'

"Absolutely not."

"Do you feel the murder was committed by one person or more than one person?" Steve Simmons asked.

"Right now, we don't know the answer to that question, but, hopefully, we will soon be able to make a decision about that," Mr. Webb responded. "I will take one more question."

"Do you know if the knife found at the crime scene was the murder weapon?" a tall man in a shirt and tie asked.

"It appears it was the murder weapon, but we need a little more time to confirm that." Mr. Webb answered. "As you would expect, we will try to find where that knife came from. That's all for now."

The anchorwoman then said, "That was Richard Webb, who is the lead investigator in the murder of Dr. Peter Mason, a prominent Atlanta physician, whose body was recently found near the Appalachian Trail north of Dahlonega. Earlier this afternoon, Trent Smith, an attorney representing Burt Atkins, made an announcement to members of the media. As you just heard during the briefing given by Richard Webb, Mr. Atkins' wife, Lori, a nurse in Dr. Mason's office, was reportedly engaged in a romantic relationship with Dr. Mason. Here is what Mr. Smith said."

A video tape of the announcement then came on the screen and Mr. Smith said, "My name is Trent Smith. I represent Mr. Burt Atkins of Atlanta. Mr. Atkins's name as been mentioned in connection with the case of Dr. Peter Mason, whose body was recently found near the Appalachian Trail in the mountains north of Dahlonega. Mr. Atkins has been considered by some to be a potential suspect in the disappearance and now apparent murder of Dr. Mason. Mr. Atkins is completely innocent of any criminal activity regarding Dr. Mason. He has retained me to insure all of his legal rights are properly observed. Mr. Atkins will cooperate with investigators assigned to this case. That is the statement which I have for you. I am not taking any questions. Thank you for coming."

The anchorwoman reappeared on the screen and said, "That ends our special coverage of this breaking story. Please watch our news at six o'clock for an update on this case."

I turned off the TV and reflected on what I had just seen. I wondered if any of the investigators had seen the parallels between Agamemnon and the Mason case. I decided to call Steve Simmons a little later and mention this matter.

The statement released by the attorney representing Burt Atkins surprised me. The fact that Atkins had hired an attorney, and hired one so soon after Dr. Mason's body was found, almost made Atkins look guilty. Why would he hire an attorney if he was innocent? Maybe he was innocent, but felt he needed to protect himself to be on the safe side.

I met with Laurel and the others at four o'clock in the practice room she had lined up. It took awhile to get organized, but we had some respectable output after an hour or so. We had to stop at six since Adam and Bob had to meet someone. We felt we had some definite promise and planned out times for two more practice sessions.

Laurel, Sergio and I went to a Chinese fast food place and had a great time. Sergio told us many jokes in his thick accent and we laughed so hard I had to frequently wipe away my tears. Once she got warmed up, Laurel proved to be quite a joke teller as well.

It would have been nice to stay longer, but we broke off so we could prepare for our morning classes.

## **Fourteen**

*It had taken the authorities longer to find the body than he had expected. He had purposely not fully covered it with forest clutter since he wanted it to be found eventually.*

*He was pleasantly surprised when the police accused Burt Atkins of the Mason murder. It was nice to have them focusing on the wrong culprit.*

*He hadn't really been nervous about killing Mason, although he was the first one to be dealt with. Still, he felt some anxiety in advance. During the actual murder process, however, the anxiety turned into exhilaration.*

*It hadn't been hard to learn that the Masons had a home in the mountains in addition to their Atlanta residence. Both locations were revealed when he ran the people-search program on his computer.*

*Through phone calls to the homes and surveillance, he determined the Mason's went to their cabin almost every weekend. That Saturday morning, he was able to follow Mason from his cabin to the parking area without being noticed. He had followed him before, and could estimate the time of Mason's return back to his car. So, it was simply a matter of timing when to meet Mason on the return leg of his hike.*

*He had posed as a veteran hiker and started down the trail at four thirty. His pack contained everything he needed. The walk was pleasant. Birds were singing, some deer crossed in front of him and he detected faint aromas of the forest. These sights, sounds and fragrances served as a serene prelude to the imminent brutality.*

*Their effect was soothing, yet strangely stimulating, and readied him for action.*

*He hadn't met any hikers before he approached Mason about five o'clock. As expected, Mason didn't recognize him in the unfamiliar context, especially in his hiking attire, without his former beard.*

*Mason had stopped to help when he pulled out his map and asked for advice about the trail ahead. He acted swiftly while Mason was fumbling with the map. Mason was easily subdued and died quickly. As he replicated the scene which unfolded in Argos centuries earlier, his mind and body performed perfectly. Once the corpse had been secured, he experienced a powerful sense of fulfillment. It had gone remarkably smoothly.*

*No one saw any of the mayhem and no one met him as he walked back to the parking area, got in his van and drove away.*

*As he had carefully steered through the tight mountain curves, he knew the others would be equally simple and satisfying. The only difficult part would be waiting for the right moments to present themselves.*

## **Fifteen**

On my way back to the dorm, I sat on the steps of the student center and called Steve Simmons on my cell phone. It was nearly nine o'clock and I felt he wasn't likely to still be in his office, but he answered the phone on the second ring.

"Steve, this is Ryan Anderson. You were certainly right when you told me something was about to break in the Mason case. Thanks for the tip."

"Don't mention it. Did you see the briefing held at three o'clock and the statement from Burt Atkins' attorney?"

"Yes. I saw you ask a couple of questions at the briefing. Were you surprised that Burt Atkins hired an attorney?"

"Not completely."

"Do you know why the police were so open about details like the robe and the knife? I'd have thought they'd want things like that kept quiet."

"Normally they are cautious about revealing such details. However, sometimes things leak out or sometimes the police have reasons they want to make details public if they feel that could be to their advantage. I don't know why they're being so open in this case."

"Steve, I called to make you aware of something in case you weren't aware of it," I said abruptly. "Are you familiar with the story of Agamemnon from ancient Greece?"

"The name sounds familiar. Oh Yeah, I saw a play by that name back in college."

"Do you remember anything about it?"

"Not much, but I remember this guy returning to his home and being killed by his wife."

"That's the general idea," I responded excitedly. "The guy was Agamemnon. He was the king who had led the Greek forces against the Trojans in the Trojan War. When he returned from the war after a long absence, his wife threw robes over him after he had bathed and killed him with a knife. Also, a line of beacons or fires between Troy and Argos was lit to signal the end of the war. This alerted Agamemnon's wife and her lover that Agamemnon was on his way home."

"I think I'm getting the picture here," Steve replied. "This sounds something like the Mason case with the robe and the knife and, I guess, the candles also. Is this just coincidence, or does it mean something?"

"I don't really know, but it certainly could."

"If there is any linkage with the Greek story, this could cast some suspicion on Trina Mason since she was a wife who had a possible motive for killing her husband," Steve ventured. "Why did Agamemnon's wife kill him?"

"It was mainly because he had sacrificed their daughter before the start of the war so the gods would provide favorable winds needed for his fleet to sail to Troy."

"Is there anything related to Agamemnon that would tend to implicate Burt Atkins?"

"I'm not aware of anything."

"Do you think anyone else has thought about the similarities between the Mason case and the Agamemnon story?"

"People who know the story of Agamemnon may see some parallels, as a few of us on campus have," I said. "In fact, we had a discussion about this in my world literature class today."

"It could be a long shot, but I may want to do a story on this angle as a supplement to the main story. If I do that, I need a source or sources. Do you think your literature professor would let me interview him or her?"

"I don't know. Her name is Dr. Sandra Chase and she's in the English Department. I suppose you could call her and see what she says. Two of my history professors know a lot about ancient Greece and they may also be sources to consider. Their names are Dr. James Chambers and Dr. Herbert Costanza."

"I think I'll call one or more of these professors to get some professional background information," Steve said. "Depending on how that goes, I may write a feature about this concept."

"I'm glad you'll be considering it."

"You certainly got my interest. We'll see where it leads," Steve replied. "Thanks, Ryan, for calling all of this to my attention. I guess we'll talk later."

As I hung up the phone, I felt a little exhilarated at Steve's interest and was anxious to see what he might put in print.

Could it be possible that Trina Mason, who had good reason to be infuriated with her husband, somehow decided to follow the example set by Clytemnestra in ancient times? Was she familiar with the story of Agamemnon? Would she have been physically capable of murdering her husband? What about Burt Atkins? What did he know about Agamemnon? He had spent time in Greece. If he had killed Dr. Mason, why would he have used a knife and a robe, and put out candles along the trail? What if someone else was involved?

There were certainly many possibilities. Maybe things would be more clear after investigators finished reviewing the evidence.

I went back to my room. Mike and a friend were just leaving to go out to eat when I arrived. Since I'd already eaten, I declined their offer to join them.

I had gotten behind with my reading assignments and tonight I was determined to make some progress in catching up. Since it was quiet in my room I decided to do some work there. Fortunately, I was able to concentrate very well and did not find my mind wandering to the Mason case, Rebecca or Monica as it often did when I was trying to study. Mike returned about midnight and was ready to go to bed since he had to get up early for crew practice.

I then went to the study lounge in my dorm. It was much quieter than normal, and I was able to work quite well without the usual distractions found in that room. By the time I finally headed back to my room at two a.m., I had managed to get current with most of my reading assignments.

The last thing I read was the beginning of *Inferno*. It started with Dante, the pilgrim, being guided into the Inferno, or hell, by Virgil, the ancient Roman writer, with assistance from Beatrice. Their first stop was Limbo. This was where virtuous souls or shades who lived and died before the time of Christ dwelt without any form of misery. It was the dwelling place for Virgil and many other persons including Homer, Ovid, Horace, Cicero, Diogenes, Thales, Anaxagoras, Ptolemy, Hippocrates, Plato, Aristotle and many others whom I recognized. I was fascinated to see how Dante, writing in the Middle Ages, was influenced by the prominent personalities of ancient times.

After leaving Limbo, Dante and Virgil began descending through lower circles of hell where they saw different classes of sinners enduring many types of excruciating torture. It was a fascinating story and I looked forward to getting back to it.

# **Sixteen**

Rebecca and I got some drinks in the student center after U.S. history and she steered me outside behind the building. We sat at a shaded table on a patio adjoining the building. I hadn't been out there before.

"Don't you just love these? We must have at least fifteen of them around campus," Rebecca said while pointing to a statue a few feet from our table of a young boy and girl playing with a rabbit.

"They're all nice. My favorite is the one with a boy and his dog."

"That is one of the best ones. My art teacher told us about these statues. They were all done by Chancellor alumni. In fact, this one right beside us was done by a woman who was in a sculpture class years ago with my art teacher when they were both undergraduates here."

"That's interesting. I don't know how anyone can create something like that. I takes real talent. Look at the expression on those kids' faces."

"I know, Ryan," Rebecca said as she put her soft hand on top of mine and squeezed gently. "They are so delicate and innocent. I've seen all of the statues, but this is my favorite."

The warmth of her hand was getting me excited as I said, "Why is that?"

She leaned closer, smiled tenderly, and said, "The girl is looking longingly at the boy, but he's playing with the rabbit and doesn't notice her."

"It looks that way," I said as I glanced at the statue.

"They remind me of me and you," Rebecca said, lowering her voice to almost a whisper. "I've been trying to get your attention, but you haven't been responding. Is this because of Monica?" she said, raising her voice to a normal tone, as she lifted her hand from mine and sat back in her chair.

I was touched and responded sheepishly, "Maybe I haven't shown it, but you have been definitely stirring my emotions inside. I'm very fond of you, but Monica and I are still very close, even though we're now in different environments and a long way apart."

"So, I've been getting through to you, have I?"

"Loud and clear. I'm a red-blooded American boy and you have definitely gotten my attention."

"That makes me feel a little better. Monica must really be special."

"Actually, I think you'd like her. I thought you had a boyfriend."

"True, but things have been changing between us." She tilted her head, stroked her silky hair and continued. "He just doesn't compare with you, Ryan."

"I don't know quite what to say, Rebecca."

"No need to say anything," she said rising from the table.

I started to respond, but she put her finger on my lips and kissed my cheek.

She then walked away a few steps, turned, smiled softly and went into the student center.

She really knew how to turn a guy on. As she disappeared my pulse raced and I felt my neck and shoulders turn red. Monica faded in significance.

I needed to collect my thoughts and was in no hurry to leave. I looked at the statue of the boy, girl, and rabbit and chuckled out loud. Rebecca had known exactly what she was doing when she brought me out here.

My cell phone rang and I heard Monica say, "Ryan, I was just sitting here thinking about you and had to give you a call."

"Oh great," I thought as she snapped me back to reality. What incredible timing. Did she somehow know what had just been going through my head?

We talked for a few minutes and, by the time we had finished, I could remember why we had been so close for as long as we had.

I'd faced a few dilemmas in my life, but this seemed to dwarf all the others. My situation reminded me of a poem I'd studied in high school about a person feeling drawn between two lovers and not knowing what to do.

Back in the dorm, I discussed my problem with Mike. After ribbing me for a couple of minutes, he turned scientific and suggested I flip a coin.

Maybe he was right. Other seemingly irresolvable decisions have been made that way by people smarter than me.

I continued to stew over this issue after Mike left to attend a meeting. Finally, I decided that it was best for me to stay in a holding pattern for awhile until something happened to tip the scales one way or the other.

## **Seventeen**

After eating with two guys from my hall, I went to the pool room in the student center. Rebecca, Sarah and I had decided to take Dr. Chambers up on his earlier invitation. They were sitting at a small square table. As I joined them, I noticed Dr. Chambers was playing someone at the table closest to where we were sitting. He waved to us as I sat down. There were three pool tables in the room and a colorful rectangular Tiffany-style lamp hung over each one. Other than the bright lights over the pool tables, the lighting in the rest of the room was dim, providing a comfortable atmosphere. It was quiet since there were no distracting video games or TV sets in the room and the few people present were talking softly.

It looked like Rebecca and Sarah had been arguing about something, but the tension evaporated when they saw me and both smiled at me when I arrived.

"Dr. Chambers said he'll join us when he finishes his game," Sarah informed me.

I wondered what they had been arguing about, but felt it best not to ask any questions in case they had been arguing about me. I had sensed a little friction between them over me in the past, but that may have just been wishful thinking on my part.

"Ryan, are you a pretty good pool player?" Rebecca asked.

"I'm not too bad. How about you?"

"I can usually hold my own pretty well."

"It sounds like I wouldn't be much competition for y'all," Sarah said acting a little sheepish. "I've only played a few times."

"I've been watching Professor Chambers as we've been sitting here," I said. "He looks quite skilled to me."

"He just looks good to me period," Sarah said with a dreamy smile. "He looks even more handsome in his casual clothes than he does in the classroom."

"Yeah, and he's not wearing a wedding ring either," Rebecca added.

"Maybe it wasn't such a good idea bringing the two of you here," I said, trying to sound serious.

"Not to worry," Sarah said. "I'm sure we'll have a good time."

Dr. Chambers finished his game, walked over to our table and said, "Mind if I join you?"

"Please do," Sarah said with an inviting smile which would get any man's attention. "You had encouraged us to meet you here sometime, and here we are."

"I'm glad you came," Dr. Chambers replied seeming very sincere. "This looks like the Odyssey team, minus one. How is your group project coming along?"

"We've all been reading the book and will soon meet to start planning our presentation," Sarah answered while fondling her necklace.

Dr. Chambers either didn't notice Sarah's come-on, or chose to ignore it and said, "That's good. The fellow I was playing with had to leave. Why don't we just talk for a few minutes and get better acquainted and then we can play some pool. Wednesday nights here are basically my informal office hours for those students who are interested."

Dr. Chambers then asked us, starting with Sarah, to tell him a little about our backgrounds, interests and reaction to his course thus far. Each of us talked for about five minutes. He listened attentively, asked occasional questions, and made various comments of approval.

He then told us more about himself to add to what he had told us in class. Among other things, he informed us that he had married a fellow graduate student at the University of Chicago before moving to Atlanta. He explained she had died of an infection following knee surgery eight years ago. While he was telling us about his wife's death he became quite somber. They had been very much in love and he felt her death should have been avoidable. However, different complications arose and she died, almost unbelievably, within two weeks of her surgery. He mentioned, with bitterness, that the now deceased Dr. Mason had been the principal physician treating his wife before she died. Dr. Chambers said he had sued Dr. Mason for malpractice but the jury had found in favor of Mason.

Dr. Chambers paused for a moment after talking about his wife, regained his composure, and said cheerfully, "I'm sorry to end on such a sad note. My wife and I had two great years together before her untimely passing. We all are going to die in our own way in our own time. I still miss her dearly, but she died eight years ago and I have had to put that in the past and live my life without her."

He rose from the table and said, "I enjoyed learning more about each of you. Now, how about some pool?"

We played rotation for about an hour and had a great time. Chambers was engaging and we had a lively conversation on many topics as we played. I played well but Rebecca played even better. Dr. Chambers was much better than both of us. He was especially skilled at bank shots and at positioning the cue ball for his next shot. Sarah was a little awkward at the game, perhaps intentionally, and Dr. Chambers gave her many tips along the way. They seemed to be quite fond of each other. I chuckled to myself a few times as Sarah launched into her Southern Belle mode when she requested help from the professor. He seemed delighted to give her assistance.

Both girls wore skimpy tops and shorts and seemed to know how to maximize the amount of skin they exposed as they twisted and stretched to make difficult shots. Dr. Chambers must have noticed, but he didn't do any obvious staring. I, however, was distracted several times and made some mistakes I shouldn't have made.

Our table, a Brunswick, was massive and very masculine, in stark contrast to our female players. Its green felt was in perfect condition and the balls ran true. It was much nicer than any table I had ever seen and was a thrill to play on.

About nine o'clock, Dr. Chambers thanked us for coming and said he had to leave. He invited us to join him for pool again whenever we could make it.

I had to get some work done, so went to the library when we left the pool room. I opened *The Odyssey* and began reading where Odysseus, continuing the telling of his adventures to Alkinoos and his followers, explained how he and his men had gone to the Underworld to consult with Teiresias upon the advice of Circe.

Odysseus did meet Teiresias and many other shades in the Underworld, including his own mother, Agamemnon, and other notable people. Odysseus hadn't been aware of Agamemnon's death and Agamemnon told Odysseus that he had been murdered by Clytemnestra and Aegisthus upon his return from Troy. I was surprised to find that reference to Agamemnon in *The Odyssey*.

After leaving the Underworld, Odysseus and his men had some other harrowing adventures and eventually, after the rest of his men had been killed, Odysseus ended up on Calypso's island where he had spent many years before coming to the land of Alkinoos.

Odysseus, with help from Alkinoos, returned to Ithaca. Athena then disguised Odysseus as a beggar so he could better decide how to deal with the suitors who had been trying to gain the affections of Penelope as they wined and dined at Odysseus' expense.

While I was anxious to know how Odysseus would confront the suitors, I was having trouble staying awake, so I quit for the night and went back to my room.

## **Eighteen**

The next afternoon, I bought a copy of the *Atlanta Herald* so I could see if there were any new developments in the Mason case. There was an article by Steve Simmons on the front page. Steve reported that police had been carefully questioning Burt Atkins, Trina Mason and other people but, thus far, there had been no arrests.

Crime scene experts were still analyzing the evidence.

A second article by Steve appeared in the interior of the paper in which he cited the parallel between the Mason case and the story of Agamemnon. Steve had obviously followed up on my suggestion and I was glad to see that. He must have contacted Dr. Chase since he used quotations from her in his story. Steve was careful to say that the similarities between the two murders were intriguing, but the similarity could be purely coincidental.

A third article by Steve concerned Burt Atkins and Trina Mason. Burt had majored in history in college and had taken a class in Greek mythology, according to a college roommate. While in the Navy, he spent much time in the Mediterranean Sea. A fellow officer had indicated that Atkins was quite knowledgeable about the ancient Greek ruins found throughout the region.

Trina Mason had majored in psychology and had not taken any classes in Greek mythology or ancient Greece. She had never been to Greece.

I was amazed at how much information Steve had collected in the short time since we had last talked. He definitely knew how to do his research. It seemed to me that Burt Atkins was beginning to look like a serious suspect. I would soon find out just how right I was.

The next morning before class I was seated near the TV in the student center when a familiar local anchorwoman announced there was breaking news in the Mason case. Burt Atkins had been arrested and charged with the murder of Dr. Peter Mason. A video tape showed Burt being taken from his home and placed in a police squad car. He was to appear in court soon for arraignment, at which time the question of bail would be discussed.

After seeing this broadcast, I went to Dr. Chambers' class. He began the session by discussing the artistic and cultural achievements of the ancient Greeks. He spent a lot of time speaking about the importance of the theatre and briefly discussed the famous playwrights. When he got to Aeschylus he asked how many of us had seen Steve Simmons' article, based upon the interview with Dr. Chase, in which the parallels between Agamemnon and the Mason case were made. Many of us acknowledged that we had read the article.

"Whether or not there is any connection between these two cases remains to be seen," Dr. Chambers said. "But, this illustrates the point, which I made on the first day of class, that learning about the past can help us better understand and deal with the issues of the present. It is for reasons such as this that we benefit from studying history."

Dr. Chambers concluded our coverage of ancient Greece at the end of class and said we would begin talking about Rome in our next session.

Rebecca and I sat under a tree on the mall for a few minutes after U.S. History.

"You're a pretty good pool player, Ryan, but I think I showed you up a little the other night."

I knew she was right, but I said, "We were quite close if you ask me."

"Say what you want, Ryan, if that makes you feel any better, but you know I'm right, my friend."

"I'd have to say you made some nice shots, but it's hard to make a judgment about who's better based on only one experience. We'll see how we perform the next time we play," I replied trying to sound confident, but knowing I would have difficulty beating her.

"Whatever."

"Say, what were you and Sarah arguing about when I got to the pool room?"

"It was just a friendly discussion."

"About what?"

"About you."

"Really?"

"Yeah, really. We can see you're really hung up on Monica, but both of us want to dump our boyfriends and go after you. Kind of dumb, huh?"

"It's nice to feel wanted, but I don't want to create any friction between the two of you."

"Don't worry. We'll work it out. Looks like she's now shifted her sights to Chambers, anyway. We get along well, and she's probably already forgotten about our little spat. I think she just wants a new boyfriend every so often and she can get new ones anytime she sets her mind to it."

"I'm sure that's true. She and Chambers did seem to hit it off quite well playing pool," I responded feeling slightly offended that I may have lost some luster in Sarah's eyes.

"Yeah, that was hard to miss. She's a brilliant actress. Maybe now I'll only have to compete with Monica," she said softly with a sly smile.

"Monica called me right after we talked behind the student center the other day. It was almost like she had been watching us. You guys are making things tough on me."

"Poor Ryan," she cooed with a playful frown. "Worse thing could happen to a guy than having two desirable females vying for his affections. I understand your dilemma and respect you for your loyalty to Monica. Just don't blame me if I keep trying to win you over. Don't forget about me, okay?"

"No way I could do that."

Rebecca shifted gears, apparently sensing I was getting uncomfortable, and we talked about casual topics for a few minutes.

*Alan Beske*

We then parted when she went to shoot some archery and I went to a practice session with the band.

# **Nineteen**

Saturday the football game was away and Sarah showed Rebecca and me some more sights around Atlanta.

After spending some time in the city, we headed north to Roswell where we stopped at a park along the Chattahoochee River. There we, surprisingly, ran into Mike, and some members of the Chancellor crew team taking their eight man boat out of the river after a practice session. Mike introduced us to his fellow rowers and they told us about their practice routine and regatta schedule. We enjoyed learning more about their sport.

Sarah then took us to the historic section of Roswell where we stopped at the Visitor's Center and then went on a guided walking tour of many historic homes which had been owned by Roswell King and other prominent citizens who had founded the city in the 1800's. We even saw a simulated Civil War military encampment on the grounds of Bulloch Hall.

We then drove from Roswell to Stone Mountain Park before going back to campus. There, we took the sky lift to the top of the mountain and got a fabulous view of downtown Atlanta.

At seven-thirty that night, we went to Hubert Hall to see Laurel and some other students perform in a piano recital.

All of the participants were quite talented. As impressive as they were, I felt Laurel clearly surpassed them all. Judging from the applause levels, it was obvious the audience shared my views.

We met Laurel in the lobby and congratulated her on her great performance. She said she had been really keyed up but was pleased with how she had done.

To celebrate, we went to a club near campus and had a good time. It was very late by the time we finally got back to our rooms.

The next morning when I got up it was raining. While I missed the warm sunshine, the rain didn't bother me since it was Sunday and I planned to put some time in at the library getting caught up on my homework.

I was finding it hard to keep up with my work load. While I basically didn't mind studying, I felt a little overwhelmed at times. I had easily gotten good grades in high school with minimal effort. Here, I expected I would get worse grades even though I put much more time into it. My parents had told me this might be the case and they seemed to be right on target.

Thus far, I had only gotten grades on two short papers and two quizzes and these had been B's and C's, unlike the solid A's I had gotten in high school. One of my problems was that I was not a fast reader and there was so much to read. Also, sometimes I had trouble staying awake while I was reading and that hurt my efficiency. All things considered, I was enjoying the academic challenges along with the other aspects of college life. Everything back in Wisconsin seemed so far away and I hardly ever thought about anything there since I was so engrossed in my new life.

I finished the last parts of *The Odyssey* where Homer tells of Odysseus' return to his home, the dramatic blood bath as the suitors were killed, and the events following the killings. It was an exciting ending to the book.

After having some lunch, I finished reading the *Inferno* section of *The Divine Comedy* and read part of the *Purgatory* section. I was intrigued by how much Odysseus' visit to the Underworld reminded me of Dante's description of *Inferno* and *Purgatory*. Also, Dante referred to many of the notable figures from ancient Greece that Homer had discussed in *The Odyssey*. I realized that I was becoming increasingly interested in ancient Greece as I learned more about it.

I was feeling quite studious and wanted to keep making progress on my mountain of homework. However, I needed a break and had a snack in the student center.

After eating, my momentum continued and I got caught up with my reading for psychology and finished an essay for English.

I left the library at two in the morning feeling good about all I had accomplished.

The next day at lunch Rebecca said, "Did you see on the news this morning that Burt Atkins has been released on bail until he comes to trial?"

"Are you kidding?" Sarah said excitedly. "I'm shocked. I hadn't expected that."

"Did they give any details on the news?" I asked.

"They showed a brief interview with his attorney who again claimed Atkins was innocent," Rebecca answered. "He said he was pleased bail had been granted and was confident Atkins' innocence would be established when the case came to trial. After the attorney spoke, the news anchorman explained that the attorney, Trent Smith, was a well known defense attorney in Atlanta."

"Trent Smith has been in the news a lot over the years. He's defended some prominent folks and gotten them off," Sarah said. "I remember my dad once said the prosecuting attorneys really fear him. He is a tall man with white hair and a white beard and he always wears white suits."

"Yeah," Rebecca said. "That's what he looked like on TV. If he's that talented, it probably explains how Burt Atkins was able to get out on bail."

"Did they say when the case may come to trial?" I asked Rebecca.

"No."

# **<u>Twenty</u>**

*He knew from his earlier research and surreptitious entry into the home that Brower lived alone and a quiver of arrows could be found in the garage. He also knew where Brower slept and was confident the house and grounds were sufficiently obscured. This advanced intelligence made his work that evening easy.*

*Brower was an incompetent attorney, and he proved to be equally incompetent in defending himself when being strangled with the thin, but strong, cord. He was weaker than would be expected for a man his size. His level of resistance was actually quite pathetic.*

*The arrow had its symbolism, surely. Also, it would keep the authorities guessing. But, he felt they would assume a burglar, maybe a deranged one, was responsible for the killing.*

*It was easy to remove the household items and move the body to the back yard. It was a dark night and the chances of anyone seeing anything suspicious were very remote.*

*The exhilaration he experienced in dispatching Brower was less intense than he had experienced with Mason. Probably, since it was the second time. Once you have killed someone, it's not quite the same when you do it again.*

*Two down and two to go. He was making progress.*

## **Twenty-One**

    Nothing eventful happened in my English composition and U.S. history classes. Rebecca went to work after history and I went back to my room. I turned on a local channel to see if there were any new developments regarding Burt Atkins. After a few minutes, the regular program was interrupted due to a breaking news item.
    An anchorman and anchorwoman jointly reported on the story. An Atlanta attorney, Clayton Brower, had been found dead that afternoon in the backyard of his home. He was lying face down with an arrow in his back. A neighbor had called police when she had spotted the body from an upstairs window of her house. Mr. Brower had been living alone in the house for the last year following a separation and divorce. His former wife and their teenage son had moved to South Carolina near the home of her parents. The house had been ransacked and burglary was the probable motive for the murder. Investigators were now on the scene and updates would be given as more information became available.
    I turned off the TV. It was unusual to hear about someone being killed by an arrow. Since Clayton Brower was an attorney, maybe Sarah's father knew something about him.
    The door opened and Mike walked in the room with David Brooks, who lived in the room next to us. I joined them for dinner and we then went to the gym and played basketball for a couple of hours. I hadn't been getting much exercise and really felt good after we finished. I'd been getting out of shape and wasn't happy about that.

None of us were in the mood for studying so we came back to David's room. He rounded up several people and we played poker until quite late. I won about thirty dollars and enjoyed that very much.

When the game broke up I still felt wide awake so I went for a walk.

The moon appeared to be full and there were only a few wispy clouds in the sky. I sat down on a bench by the mall where I had a spectacular view of the moon over the steeple of the chapel, framed by tree branches. It was a perfect photographic opportunity for someone with the right talent and equipment.

The lawn in front of me was amazingly bright and a soft breeze cooled my face. I felt more relaxed than I had in weeks and sat there for about twenty minutes, thinking about nothing in particular, before going back to my room.

The next day, I had an appointment with Dr. Wilkens. She was working on her computer as I knocked. She greeted me cordially and put me at ease immediately. We sat at her round table after, as in my prior visit, she had removed the materials which had been stacked on it. She was wearing a pink dress, which fit her perfectly, and looked great.

"Ryan, it's good to see you. I'm feeling especially good today since I just learned a grant application which I worked so hard on has been approved. If I was grading papers today, I'd probably give everyone an A."

"Congratulations. I don't have anything for you to grade, but it sounds like it might be a good day to show you the outline for my paper about the Peter Mason murder."

"Your timing is probably very appropriate," she said smiling as she leaned closer to me, brushing her hand against mine as she took my paper. "Let me take a look at what you've got."

She read my outline, asked a few questions and made two suggestions.

"Ryan, if you make those changes, you have the basic structure for a first rate paper. I know it's an unusual topic for my class, but it will be a good experience for you. I'm confident you'll do well with it and will look forward to seeing your end result."

"Thanks for your encouragement. And thanks for lining up my visit with Mr. White. The reporter he introduced me to, Steve Simmons, has been supportive so far and will do what he can to help me with the paper."

"I'm glad that worked out. Stop back to see me if you have any questions later."

"Okay, I'll do that if I need some help downstream."

I thought she may have been flirting with me during my first trip to her office. This time there was no doubt in my mind. I wasn't sure what to think. While I was tempted to see where this could lead, I decided it was best to give her no encouragement.

Later in the afternoon I met with Rebecca, Sarah and Tyler in the student center to discuss our group project.

After we all sat down and got organized, I asked, "Did any of you hear about the attorney, Clayton Brower, who was found dead in his yard with an arrow in his back?"

"Yes, wasn't that strange?" Rebecca said. "You don't see too many people being killed by arrows any more."

"I heard about it and even called Daddy to see if he knew Mr. Brower," Sarah said. "He met Brower in a couple of trials, but didn't know him well. Daddy said Brower did a lot of trial work and he handled various types of personal injury and defense cases. He used to have a drinking problem and made some blunders along the way as a result, but seemed to be functioning effectively the last year or two after he apparently stopped drinking."

"It sounded like he might have been killed by a burglar," I said.

"Probably so, although it very strange with the arrow and all," Sarah replied.

"Has everyone finished reading the book?" Sarah asked.

"I just finished re-reading it this morning," Tyler responded. "Odysseus and Telemachus really got even with the suitors at the end."

"I finished it," I said. "Great story."

"It was good," Rebecca said. "I liked how Homer had Athena and the other gods and goddesses interacting with the mortals. I also liked it when Odysseus, disguised as the old man, strung the bow and shot his arrow through the rings in all of the axes."

"I'm not surprised you liked that part." I said to Rebecca. "What did you think about Odysseus killing all of those men with his bow and arrows?"

"Quite a finale."

"When I heard about the attorney being killed by an arrow, it reminded me of Odysseus' killing of the suitors," Sarah said.

"Good point," Rebecca said. "I hadn't thought about that."

"Well anyway," Sarah said, "we need to decide how to approach our assignment."

We then got to work. By the time we had finished, we had a detailed outline of our class presentation and everyone had research assignments concerning our supplementary sources.

## **Twenty-Two**

The next day, Rebecca, Sarah and I went to the student center to watch a press conference about the Clayton Brower murder. The police spokesman was Norman Cooley. He stated that an intruder had apparently entered Brower's bedroom while he was sleeping and strangled him with a nylon cord found beside the bed. There were signs of a struggle and abrasions from the cord were found on Brower's neck. Preliminary evidence indicated that the killer had taken an arrow from an archery set in the garage and rammed the arrow in Brower's back after he was dead, before dragging the body to the back yard. Burglary appeared to be the motive since some items of value had been taken. After providing this information, Cooley opened the meeting to questions.

A familiar TV newswoman asked, "Do you have any clues as to why the murderer put the arrow in Mr. Brower's dead body and moved it to the yard? That seems very bizarre."

"It is bizarre," Cooley answered. "Killers or other criminals sometimes have trademarks or try to make various statements at crime scenes. Maybe that's what happened here."

"If the killer was, in fact, leaving some kind of a trademark, are there any similar crimes which resemble this one?" Steve Simmons asked.

"At this point we haven't identified anything like this," Cooley answered. "But, we are still checking to see what might have happened anywhere in the country."

"What kinds of items were stolen?" a young male reporter with a yellow tie asked.

"Some computer equipment, stereo equipment and TV sets were missing. There may have been more items stolen that we are not aware of yet."

"Is it possible Mr. Brower removed those items himself before he was murdered?" a stocky man asked.

"That's not likely. They appeared to have been removed in haste, presumably by the person who killed Mr. Brower."

"Did any neighbors see or hear anything which might help solve the case?" Steve Simmons asked.

"Not that we've been able to determine so far," Cooley answered. "Much of Mr. Brower's house and driveway are obscured behind trees and bushes. For that reason and since the crime apparently happened late at night, an intruder could have gone undetected for quite some time."

"Did Mr. Brower live alone in the house?" a tall woman in a red dress asked.

"Yes, his former wife and son had moved out about a year ago," Cooley replied.

"Are there any suspects in this case?" the stocky man asked.

"None at this point. We are still gathering and analyzing evidence and are interviewing many people who may be able to provide useful information. Thank you for coming. That's all we have time for now."

With that remark, Cooley abruptly ended the news conference even though reporters tried to ask more questions as he left the room.

"This whole thing is so strange," Rebecca said.

"I know," Sarah responded. "Why would anyone push an arrow in someone's back after he was already dead?"

"It does make you wonder" I said in agreement.

"Maybe it was some serial killer trying to make a statement," Rebecca said speculatively, "It seems unlikely to me, though. Maybe there is some other explanation."

"A lot of robberies are committed by people trying to get money to buy drugs," I replied. "Maybe that's what happened here."

"Someone like that maybe would steal electronic items, because they may be easier to convert to cash than other household goods," Rebecca said.

"If it was a person with a drug problem, he could have been capable of doing weird things, such as using the arrow," Sarah speculated. "Maybe he would have done something like that to make it look like a serial killer was the culprit."

"That's possible," Rebecca replied. "Maybe the killer was not a burglar, but someone else who had a reason to want Brower dead."

"That could be," I said. "Maybe, like Dr. Mason, he was having an affair with someone and the husband got even,"

"If he was not a good lawyer, as my Daddy said," Sarah stated, "maybe, some disgruntled client sought revenge."

"Your dad also heard that he had, or formerly had, a drinking problem," Rebecca added. "People with drinking problems sometimes get into financial trouble. Maybe he was killed because he failed to repay some loan shark."

"Divorces are sometimes messy," I said. "Maybe his former wife had something to do with his murder."

"Hey," I said thinking it was time to change the subject. "It's Wednesday. Should we play pool with Dr. Chambers again?"

"Of course," Sarah said sounding very upbeat. "I'm interested. I might even develop some skill in the game if I had some more practice."

"I smell romance brewing," Rebecca said, chiding Sarah. "Count me in."

## **Twenty-Three**

Sarah, Rebecca and Dr. Chambers were having a lively conversation at a small table in the pool room when I arrived at six thirty.

"Ryan, there you are," Sarah said. "We were having a good laugh since Rebecca and I have just called one of Dr. Chambers' theories into question."

"That's right, Ryan," Dr. Chambers said smiling. "I was telling your charming friends that men, in my experience, are more likely to be early than women for scheduled events. They told me you all were planning to be here at six thirty and they were here a few minutes before that. I guess my theory may have to be reexamined."

"Sorry to mess things up," I replied.

"Anyway, I'm glad to see all of you here again," Dr. Chambers said sincerely. "We can play pool shortly, but it would be nice if we could visit a little while first. You are all freshmen. How are you liking it here at Chancellor so far?"

"It's everything I had expected," Sarah said eagerly. "I've thought about coming here for years and am really enjoying it. You and the other professors are keeping us pretty busy, but that's not surprising to me."

"It's been great for me so far," Rebecca said. "I'm really enjoying my classes and have met some great people."

"For me, it's a major change from high school, but I'm glad I'm here," I added.

We talked for several minutes as Dr. Chambers asked us various questions. In the course of the conversation, all of us mentioned that we planned to major in history.

"This is my lucky night to be spending it with three history majors," Dr. Chambers said sounding very pleased. "How are things going with your presentation on *The Odyssey*?"

"We're working hard on it and hope to do a good job," Sarah answered.

"We all really liked the book and that will make our project quite interesting," I said. "It's so well written and the climax when Odysseus, Telemachus and their loyal helpers killed all of the suitors was quite exciting."

"It was violent, but was a thrilling ending to the story," Rebecca added. "Actually we even thought of *The Odyssey* when we heard about the attorney who was found with an arrow in his back."

"That's an interesting observation," Dr Chambers said. By the way, I knew Clayton Brower, so I have been following the news about him. Last week I told you there was a trial following my wife's death. Clayton Brower represented me in that trial, although his quality of representation left much to be desired. As I told you last week, Dr. Mason was in that same trial. I find it amazing that both of them have now come to violent deaths. Well, enough of this morbid talk about violence. Can I interest you all in some pool tonight?"

We played until eight o'clock when Dr. Chambers had to leave. He was friendly and talkative and made some fantastic shots. Sarah played much better than last week, which reinforced my theory that she had been purposely under-performing to get Chambers' attention. However, the two of them seemed to relate to each other very well, in spite of her improved playing performance.

Sarah's acting talent was obvious, and it was fun watching her in action.

Rebecca played well again, but my game was a little off. We had a good time and it was a lot more fun than studying.

The three of us sat down at a table and talked for awhile after Chambers left. Then Sarah said, "Hey y'all, we've got Clayton Brower down at the morgue. Would you like to go take a look at him?"

"Are you serious?" Rebecca asked.

"Yeah. What do you say? Should we go?"

"Why not?" I responded, not sure that I really wanted to see a dead body.

"Let's go," Rebecca said eagerly.

Sarah showed us the office area where she worked and then we went into the morgue.

"Someone is supposed to be here, but they must have stepped away," Sarah said. "I think it will be okay if we just help ourselves."

She scanned some labels on the wall of metal compartments and said, "Here he is," as she pulled out one of the long drawers. She folded back a sheet and we found ourselves staring at a very dead Clayton Brower.

"Ugh...not a pleasant sight," Rebecca said softly.

My stomach churned a little. Brower was very pale. Seeing him lying there made me, somehow, think of the inhabitants of *Inferno*.

"I'm not going to turn him over to see where the arrow was in his back, but look at the abrasions around his neck," Sarah said with authority. "It makes me think of something I recently saw on TV."

"I see the marks," Rebecca said. "Man, I'm glad I don't have to do this for a living."

"I seldom get back here," Sarah said intently, "but this place fascinates me. Seen enough?"

"More than enough," I answered.

"Okay," Sarah said as she pulled the sheet back in place and pushed the drawer closed with a soft clunk. "Want to take a look at any other bodies while we're here?"

"That's enough for one night," Rebecca answered.

We left and went back to campus. Sarah was quite talkative, but Rebecca and I didn't say much. I felt uneasy, but, for some reason, was glad that we had a chance to see Brower's body. However, I knew I wouldn't be in any hurry to see another corpse.

## **Twenty-Four**

At five o'clock the next afternoon, I joined Laurel, Adam, Bob and Sergio for another practice session. We had decided to call ourselves Proud Phoenix, taken from the notion that Atlanta rose from the ashes like the mythical bird after Sherman's army paid its devastating visit.

We played remarkably well together and, while I held my own, I was probably the least talented of the group. They were all superior to anyone I had played with in the past.

After a couple of hours, we went out for some Italian food. While Laurel as the lone female was heavily outnumbered, she defended herself well as we tried to argue that males were better decision makers than females. Each time one of us made a seemingly good point, Laurel countered with a convincing response.

We then spent a long time telling jokes. I told the only two jokes I could remember and they didn't go over too well. Everyone contributed, but Sergio proved that he was a master comedian compared to the rest of us. He had us all wiping our eyes and slapping the table repeatedly. In his finale joke, while waving his arms, Sergio knocked Adam's half-full plate in Laurel's lap. We really cracked up as Laurel flung some pasta and tomato fragments back at Sergio.

We finally stopped laughing and decided to come to the restaurant again sometime if they would allow us to return.

"You really are into this forensics stuff," Rebecca said to Sarah as we were having lunch on the mall the next day.

"I guess it must be pretty obvious," Sarah replied. "Did y'all enjoy our trip to the morgue?"

"Enjoy wouldn't be the right word," Rebecca replied, "but it did get me more interested in Brower's murder."

"Same here. By the way, I called Steve Simmons this morning. He said the police think the murderer may have copied a crime that was covered on one of the reality TV programs recently. In that case, a burglar stuck a knife in a housewife's back and dragged her to her back yard after he had smothered her. According to Steve, the police are pretty convinced Brower was killed by a burglar who was deranged in some way or under the influence of drugs. They don't seem to suspect his wife, son or anyone else."

"I just remembered what Dr. Chambers told us the other night," Rebecca said. "Both Peter Mason and Clayton Brower were in the malpractice trial following the death of Chambers' wife. Isn't that something?"

"It's amazing," Sarah replied.

That evening, Mike and I went to a party at an apartment near campus. It was pretty lively and many people came and went. I played my guitar for awhile and people seemed to enjoy my music. We made several new friends, but drank more than we should have.

Saturday I didn't feel up to par when I went to the football game with Mike and some guys from our hall. It was an exciting game and we won due to a lucky touchdown. By the time the game was over, I had recovered and was ready to celebrate. So, when we went from the stadium to a post-game party I was ready to make a long night of it.

The next couple of weeks went by smoothly. There was plenty of school work, but I had enough spare time to have lunch with Rebecca and Sarah regularly, play pool on Wednesday nights and practice with Proud Phoenix. Weekends were devoted to football games and parties, but not too much studying.

I buckled down for midterms and they were exhausting. I prepared hard for each test. Most of them focused on essays and short answers, but they usually had some true-false and multiple choice questions. My professors seemed to be skilled in making the multiple choice questions harder than the essay questions and that surprised me. The fingers on my right hand were sore from all of the writing by the time I finished the last exam. I felt I had done reasonably well, but didn't feel comfortable with my psychology test.

During the midterm period, I had no time to think about the women in my life, my family, murder cases or anything non-academic in nature.

Rebecca, Sarah and I compared notes at lunch after our tests were over and we had gotten our results. They both got all A's and B's. I got B's, but, unfortunately, only got a D+ in psychology.

"How could you get a D+ in psychology? That took some doing," Rebecca blurted out as she arched her eyebrows.

"Yeah, Ryan. You better get your act together," Sarah added, rubbing it in.

"Okay guys, back off," I responded trying to appear annoyed, but smiling. "Don't count me out yet. I'll do fine on the final."

"Well, it's good to be done with mid terms," Sarah concluded. "Hey, are we playing pool tonight?"

"Sure," Rebecca added. "We all deserve a break."

"Sounds good," I added.

"Good, we can meet there at six thirty," Sarah said.

"Have you thought about the classes you'd like to take next semester?" Rebecca asked. "Registration starts in a few days. Maybe we could take a class or two together again."

"I've started thinking about next term," Sarah said. "Dr. Chambers will be teaching his Greek mythology class. Why don't we all sign up for that. It's at ten o'clock and we could continue to have lunch together after his class."

"I'm interested," Rebecca replied.

"Me too," I said.

"Wonderful," Sarah said. "Do you know what else you may want to take?"

"Our U.S. history course is a two course sequence," Rebecca said. "I'd like to take the next course which covers from eighteen hundred through the present. Ryan, are you game?"

"Yeah." I replied. "I guess we can put up with Costanza for another semester."

"What else are you thinking about taking, Sarah?" I asked.

"Since I'm interested in a legal career and forensics, I want to take criminology. I'll also probably take biology, world politics, and an introduction to theater class."

"Those sound good, especially the criminology," I said. "These murders have gotten me interested in anything to do with crime. Can I take the criminology class with you?"

"That'd be great. Rebecca, why don't you join us?"

"I'd like to, but probably won't be able to take it next term," she said a little tentatively. "But if I don't take it, I hope you two will behave yourselves, when I'm not around."

"Of course we'd be on our best behavior," Sarah replied. "And, I hope you two will also be on your best behavior in your second U.S. history class together."

Trying to change the subject I said, "Rebecca, what else might you take next term?"

"I'll probably try to take physics, astronomy and sociology in addition to the two history classes. What about you, Ryan?"

"Besides the history classes and criminology, I'll probably try to take creative writing, and anthropology. Creative writing is being taught by professor Wilkens, who's now teaching my English composition class. She's really doing a good job with that."

"I can imagine," Rebecca said sarcastically. "A girl from my hall is in your class and she pointed Wilkens out to me last week...Pretty sexy for a forty-something woman!"

"Yeah, and she kind of likes me too."

"My, don't you sound proud today," Rebecca responded while adjusting her earring. "She's a little old for you, don't you think?"

"Maybe, but I've heard some interesting stories about older women."

"Don't kid yourself, buster," Sarah said as she patted my shoulder. "They can't compare with people your own age."

"Yeah, Ryan," Rebecca added, stroking my other shoulder. "Monica might meet her match if we ever decide to shed our less-than-perfect boyfriends."

## **Twenty-Five**

We all arrived at six thirty and sat at our normal table. Dr. Chambers was playing pool with an older gentleman, who seemed to be a faculty member and he waved when he saw us sit down. A few minutes later Dr. Chambers and the other gentlemen walked over to our table when they had finished their game.

"Dr. Wilson, I'd like to have you meet three of the best students in my Western civilization class," Dr. Chambers said cheerfully.

We all stood up and Dr. Chambers continued. "They are Sarah Flemming, Rebecca Chan and Ryan Anderson." We shook Dr. Wilson's hand as we were being introduced. "Dr. Wilson is the head of our History Department and has been a distinguished member of the Chancellor faculty for over thirty years."

"I'm very pleased to meet all of you," Dr. Wilson said warmly. "Every once in awhile, Dr. Chambers talks me into a few games of pool. We always have a good time, despite the fact that he always prevails. I do find it very relaxing, however. Have any of you managed to best him at this game yet?"

"No, but we're trying hard," Sarah said.

"Well, Dr. Chambers is difficult to beat in pool and he is also one of our most admired faculty members. He is a very talented academician and is loved by his students. We are certainly delighted to have him in our department. He makes us all look good."

"Thanks for your kind words, Dr. Wilson, but if you say any more, I'll start to blush," Dr. Chambers said actually sounding a little embarrassed. "I should point out, Dr. Wilson, that all three of these students are planning to major in history."

"That's delightful," Dr. Wilson said as he looked at us with a broad smile. "We have a very respected program, thanks to excellent professors such as Dr. Chambers, Dr. Costanza and many others, which is consistently highly ranked at both the undergraduate and graduate levels. Much of our strength has also come from the caliber of our students and our distinguished alumni. Well, enough of that. I'm afraid I have a meeting to attend and must leave now. I'm glad we had this chance to meet each other. Please feel free to contact me, Dr. Chambers, or other members of our department whenever we can be of help. Good luck to all of you."

We all said goodbye to Dr. Wilson, sat down and Dr. Chambers said, "Dr. Wilson is right about the enviable stature of our program and he deserves most of the credit. He's one of the most recognized historians in the country and serves on numerous distinguished professional boards and commissions."

"He's very impressive," Sarah said. "I'm glad we were able to meet him."

"I'm glad too," Dr. Chambers replied. "I must admit it wasn't an accidental meeting. Dr. Wilson is usually very busy, but he was interested in coming here tonight when I told him you three might be present. He is always anxious to meet any of our history majors. By the way, congratulations on your midterm results. You all did quite well, Sarah especially, since she had the second highest score in the class."

"Is that right?" Sarah exclaimed. "That's nice to hear. I'm assuming that Tyler got the top score. Is that right?"

"You're right there," Dr. Chambers replied. "I don't think anyone would be surprised at that."

"Dr. Chambers, all three of us are hoping to take your Greek mythology class next semester," Sarah said. "We're interested in that field."

"I'm glad to hear that. I'll welcome having you in another of my classes."

A table then opened. We played several games of pool and all had a good time as we talked about, the weather, the Atlanta Braves, friction in the Middle East, vanishing rain forests and other random topics which seemed somehow to naturally flow from one to the next. All of us were playing better than normal and that made it even more enjoyable. As usual, Sarah and Dr. Chambers related to each other very well.

As I sat down in my psychology class the next day I resolved to buckle down since I felt a strong need to bring my grade up by the end of the semester. Our professor, Dr. Sylvia Applegate, spent the session discussing abnormal psychology and I found that to be quite interesting, in contrast to much of the material we had covered earlier. That was encouraging. As I sat there, I convinced myself I could raise my grade to a C or B by the end of the term.

## **<u>Twenty-Six</u>**

The next day, during Dr. Costanza's class he asked for some volunteers to put notices around campus announcing an upcoming lecture by a distinguished history professor from Princeton. Rebecca and I agreed to help and we followed him to his office after class to get the notices. We felt it wouldn't hurt our grades any if we tried to be helpful.

"Thanks for volunteering," Dr. Costanza said as we entered his office. "Please sit down for a few minutes. I like the way both of you have been participating in class. How are you liking U.S. history so far?"

He was obviously trying to show some warmth toward us, which contrasted drastically with his normal intimidating posture. This put me at ease somewhat, but I still felt uncomfortable. As we answered his question, he listened intently and shifted his dark eyes between Rebecca and me as we talked.

After we had talked for a few minutes, he pulled a folder from a file cabinet and gave it to me saying, "Here are the notices we talked about. Please try to get them on bulletin boards and other logical places by next Tuesday. This is the first in a four person guest lecturer series. I'd appreciate it if you could help by posting the other notices for the talks next semester."

"We can do that," Rebecca answered.

"That would be nice of you," Dr. Costanza replied. "Thanks for your help. I'll contact you in advance of the future distributions."

Rebecca and I then went to the student center to wait for a meeting with Sarah and Tyler. As we sat down, Rebecca said, "He was trying to be nice, but I was still nervous with him."

"I feel the same way."

We talked for a few minutes and then Sarah and Tyler joined us. After some casual conversation, Sarah got us into focus when she said, "Let's see where we stand on *The Odyssey*. We all had our assignments so I suggest each of us take a few minutes to tell what will be addressed in our portion of the presentation."

"We're in good shape," Sarah said after we had all finished giving our input. "We sounded pretty convincing as far as I'm concerned. Next we need to make our transitions a little smoother."

Sarah then guided us for another thirty minutes as we made some nice improvements in our planned presentation.

We felt like our session was productive and all went out for a Chinese dinner, followed by a few games of pool at the student center. I enjoyed the opportunity to get to know Tyler better. He was in good spirits and seemed glad to spend some time socializing with us.

The next day was Saturday and our football game was away. Sarah wanted to take a look at Clayton Brower's house, so Rebecca and I went with her. Sarah had gotten a map from the internet.

We drove by the house slowly, turned around, returned and parked out front. The neighborhood was quite mature and very wooded. Brower's home, as well of those of his neighbors, was on a large lot. His driveway was curved and, from the road where we were parked, you couldn't see the entrance to the garage due to the trees and shrubs.

It looked like the police were still treating the property as a crime scene since they had strung yellow tape between trees around the perimeter of the lot.

We hadn't been able to see Brower's back yard from the street as we drove by. After sitting in the car for a minute, Sarah said, "Want to explore a little?"

"The cops probably don't want us messing around," Rebecca responded. "Can your dad get us off the hook if we get in trouble?"

"Come on," Sarah replied. "We'll just take a quick look and will be gone before anyone sees us."

"Since we're here, let's take a closer look," I said trying to sound macho, but I felt a little uneasy going under the tape barrier.

We walked around the side of the house and took a footpath which led us into the back yard after we ducked under another crime scene tape.

The backyard was small compared with the front yard, and was framed by a neatly trimmed hedge. We were a little nervous about being where we didn't belong and did not venture very far onto the grass. I tried to visualize Brower's body lying face down somewhere on the lawn with an arrow in his back. I felt uncomfortable standing there.

We then carefully walked back to the car, got in, and I said, "The layout is similar to what I had imagined based on the news reports. It looks like the murderer could have parked in the driveway and later carried a body to the back yard in the dark without being seen by anyone."

"Yes," Rebecca said. "And, since the houses are fairly far apart, he probably wouldn't have been heard by anyone either if he made any noise."

"Seeing this house really makes one wonder what happened that night when Brower was killed," Sarah said. "I'm getting goose bumps just being here. Well, I guess we've seen enough so we'll head back to campus."

As Sarah parked the car she said, "By the way, if you're not going home for Thanksgiving my parents and I would like to have you join us for dinner at our place in the mountains."

"That sounds like fun since I can't afford to make the trip home," Rebecca replied.

"I won't be able to go home either and would like to come," I said. "I'd enjoy seeing your parents again."

"Great. I'm glad you'll be able to make it. My brother should be there too and I'd like to have you meet him."

That evening I went to a party with Mike and two other friends from my dorm. I had asked Rebecca and Sarah if they would like to join us, but they both were going out with their boyfriends.

I continued to keep well-occupied with school work, Proud Phoenix and some socializing, and the days went by fast. Before I realized it, Thanksgiving was here. I was pleased with how all of my classes, except for psychology, had been going, and Dr. Wilkins had been very satisfied with my paper on the Mason case, which I managed to complete a week before the deadline. I had really gotten into my college routine and was relishing all aspects of it, despite the fact that I wasn't getting enough sleep most of the time. After all that had been going on, I felt a little exhausted and welcomed the opportunity to take a short break.

## **Twenty-Seven**

Rebecca rode with me to the Flemming's house. Sarah had given me a map putting us on a route north from Atlanta on some scenic two lane roads. It was nice to get away from the city and experience more of rural Georgia. The day was sunny and it was about sixty-five degrees. Most of the homes along the roads were small and well-kept and there was almost no litter to detract from the pleasing landscape. We saw a few antique shops and an old general store as the roads curved through the hills.

Sarah had told us some things about the Big Canoe development where her parent's home was located. It was a large gated community covering several mountains. Homes were dispersed along wooded roads and had to meet architectural standards which complemented the natural environment. Many of the residents were retired business and professional people, but the development was also becoming popular with younger families. Many of the homeowners, as in the case of the Flemmings, were part time residents who used their homes on weekends or for vacations and holidays.

"It looks like we're here," I said as I pulled off the highway and drove down a quiet tree-shrouded road up to a security gate.

A friendly attendant said we were expected and gave me a visitor's pass to hang from my rear view mirror. She also gave us a map and showed us how to get to the proper road.

We left the entrance and followed a winding road, soon going through a picturesque covered bridge.

"I feel like we're in a national park," Rebecca said. "We're really in quite a forest and everything is so well kept. There's even a Smoky the Bear sign over here," she said as she pointed to the side of the road.

"Very nice," I replied, craning my neck to look in all directions as I rounded a curve. "I like this place. You really are away from all of the congestion of the city."

We soon passed the entrance to the golf club and saw some of the holes rimming a beautiful lake.

"That must be where Sarah plays tennis," Rebecca said gesturing to her right. "She said they have a large fitness center, swimming complex and marina. Nice place to relax, I must say."

"I could adjust to living here in about two seconds."

Rebecca gave me directions using the map as we took a steep road up one of the mountains. We kept going higher and higher and saw numerous nice homes nestled in the trees, many of them perched on the sides of the mountain.

"These builders must have some special talents to be able to put these homes on such steep lots," Rebecca exclaimed. "Hey, slow down, look at those deer."

"They certainly don't seem to be very afraid of us. What a sight," I replied trying to look at three deer at the side of the road while negotiating a sharp upward curve.

"I think we've reached the top of the mountain," Rebecca said breathlessly. "You can see forever from up here. There's the number we're looking for. Pull into the driveway on your right."

"Hello," Mr. Flemming said heartily as he met us at the front door. "I'm glad you were able to find us alright."

"It was quite a drive getting all the way up here," Rebecca said. "What a spectacular area."

"This is really something," I added. "We even saw a few deer. They seemed very tame."

"We have plenty of them, along with wild turkeys, some bears and other animals. They give the place a nice rustic character. Please join the rest of us in the living room."

"Rebecca and Ryan, I'd like to have you meet Judge Franklin Peters and his wife Elizabeth," Mr. Flemming said as we entered the living room.

"Ryan Anderson," I said as I shook hands with the judge and his wife.

"Hi, I'm Rebecca Chan," Rebecca said also shaking their hands. "It's a pleasure meeting you."

"Doris and I have been friends with the Peters for over twenty years and we often get together on holidays or other special occasions," Mr. Flemming said. "Rebecca and Ryan are friends of Sarah's at Chancellor," he added addressing Judge and Mrs. Peters. "We're happy they could join us for Thanksgiving since they won't have a chance to be at home with their families."

Mrs. Flemming gave both Rebecca and me a hug and welcomed us.

"Sarah and Charles, come join us," Mr. Flemming said.

"Hi guys," Sarah said to Rebecca and me. "This is my big brother, Charles. He came home from Boston for the holiday. Charles, please meet Rebecca and Ryan. They are freshmen at Chancellor and we are the best of friends."

"It's a pleasure meeting both of you," Charles said jovially as he shook our hands. "I've heard some good things about you from Sarah."

I liked Charles instantly. He was tall and a little heavy and reminded me of a friendly teddy bear who could have hosted a children's TV program.

"It's nice meeting you," Rebecca said. "We've got many good things to say about Sarah also."

"Yeah, Sarah has been great and she has really helped us learn more about Atlanta," I said. "Are you going to school in Boston?"

"Yes, I'm a junior at MIT," Charles replied. "Surprisingly, I might even graduate next year."

"Don't let his 'aw shucks' manner fool you guys," Sarah laughed. "He just missed 1600 on his SAT."

"Just luck, I assure you," Charles replied with a funny grin.

"Sarah, we won't eat for about thirty minutes and Dad and I have to review something with the Peters before we eat," Mrs. Flemming said. "Why don't the four of you relax on the deck for awhile. I left some lemonade on the table. I'll call you when we're ready to sit down."

"Okay Mom," Sarah replied. Then, turning to Rebecca and me she said, "This way."

While it was late November, it was warm enough to sit comfortably outside. This prompted me to say, "The weather in Georgia is hard to beat. We would never enjoy this temperature in Wisconsin at Thanksgiving time."

"It's not this nice in Boston either this time of the year," Charles added. "The winters there are a little hard on us Southern boys."

Sarah filled our glasses and said, "Cheers" as she raised her glass. "Sorry I can't offer you something a little stronger."

"Your view from here is awesome," Rebecca exclaimed. "I love how you can see the lake way down there and all the mountains."

"It still looks great even though most of the leaves have fallen," I added.

"I'm glad you like it," Sarah said. "This is a very favorite place for me. The view is wonderful year round, especially when the leaves are in full color. I love to sit out here with a cup of tea and a good book whenever I get the chance. It's hard to get more relaxed than that."

The four of us talked until we were called to the table. I could see why Sarah was so fond of spending time on that deck. It was such a tranquil setting, and the view was hard to beat.

Once we all sat down, Mr. Flemming led us in a short prayer. After he had finished, he said "Bon appetit."

The food was delicious and included turkey, ham, sweet potatoes, dressing, cranberries, green beans, carrots and a tasty pumpkin pie covered with whipped cream for desert.

The meal was purely traditional and I knew it would be very close to what my mother had prepared back home. We had a lively conversation as we ate and everyone took an active part.

As we ate, I noticed it seemed like we were in a comfortable mountain lodge. There were exposed beams in the ceiling and numerous rugs, pictures and wall hangings featured moose, bear and fish. I especially liked the distressed pine flooring.

While we were having desert, Judge Peters was very talkative and seemed more like a friendly uncle than a judge.

After he monopolized the conversation for about ten minutes, Sarah's mother asked, "Sarah, have you thought about what courses you'll be taking next semester?"

"Yes, I was able to confirm everything I applied for. I'll be taking Greek mythology, biology, world politics, criminology and introduction to theater. Rebecca and Ryan will be in Greek mythology with me and Ryan will be taking the criminology course."

"Those all sound interesting," Sarah's dad said. "The criminology class may be particularly relevant given your interest in the legal profession."

"Yeah, I'm especially looking forward to that one."

"Ryan, so you are also taking the criminology class," Sarah's dad said. "I take it you also have some interest in that field."

"Yes, and I've have gotten even more interested lately as a result of the mysterious murders of Dr. Peter Mason and attorney Clayton Brower."

"When you and Rebecca and Sarah visited us several weeks ago Sarah said you were going to write a paper about the Mason case for a class project," Sarah's mother said addressing me. "How did that turn out?"

"It was an interesting project for me and my professor was pleased with the end result. I got a lot of help from Steve Simmons, the *Atlanta Herald* reporter who focused on the case."

"Simmons is a real veteran," Sarah's dad said. "If a story in Atlanta has any significance, he's the person who seems to be front and center for the Herald."

"Simmons has covered some of the trials which I handled," Judge Peters added. "He's very aggressive and always seems to research his stories thoroughly. Regarding your other comment, I've presided over trials involving Clayton Brower and Peter Mason. Their deaths were tragic."

"Both murders were definitely very shocking," Sarah's dad said. "I don't believe you'll be handling the Burt Atkins trial will you judge? Won't that be heard by Ted Wallace?"

"Yes, Ted's got that one," Judge Peters replied. "That really is an unusual case."

"It really is," Sarah's dad replied.

"Doris, everything was absolutely delicious," Mrs. Peters said. "You are such a fabulous cook."

"It was exquisite," Judge Peters echoed. "As usual, I over indulged, but I wouldn't have missed your wonderful cooking for anything."

The rest of us also offered assorted compliments.

After we got up from the table, Mr. Flemming invited everyone down to the lower level since he wanted to show us a huge 50's-looking juke box he had gotten a few days earlier. He had fun showing us how it worked using a fancy remote control unit.

While music flowed from the juke box, most of us played pool on Mr. Flemming's ornate pool table. It looked like it had come from a saloon in the old West. Sarah seemed right at home and made some great shots. She was obviously a much better natural player than she had led us to believe back at the student center.

Sarah smiled at me and Rebecca after sinking an ultra thin cut and said, "Did you like that one?"

"You sure had us fooled!" Rebecca exclaimed.

"Don't tell me my daughter has been sandbagging again," Mr. Flemming said with a smirk.

"She fooled me once," Judge Peters said laughing. "It sounds like she got you too."

"We knew she was a good actress," I said. "This proves it. Sarah, you really have been keeping your talent hidden from us." While I was tempted to add "and from Dr. Chambers," I kept silent.

A little later Sarah's mother and Mrs. Peters came down from the kitchen. They wanted to play black jack, so we put up our cues and all sat around a large round table.

Mrs. Flemming explained that she had worked as a dealer in Las Vegas between her undergraduate and graduate schooling and had never gotten the game out of her system. She entertained us with some stories from her casino days and then served as our dealer for about an hour.

She was an elegant Southern woman from all outward appearances, but it was fascinating to watch her revert back to the role which she had performed long ago.

By the time we had finished, Rebecca had the biggest pile of chips. Mr. Flemming and the judge acted a little frustrated at the outcome, but I could tell they enjoyed seeing her play so well.

Following the game, Rebecca and I said our goodbyes. On our drive back we didn't speak much. It had been a great day. I felt very rested and was full from our meal a few hours earlier. I sensed Rebecca was quiet for the same reasons.

## **Twenty-Eight**

*Judge Peters didn't know what hit him. Three quick shots and he collapsed to the concrete floor. He probably died instantly. The silencer nicely muffled the sounds.*

*It took him only a few seconds to lift the body into his van and cover it with the dark tarp. There were no witnesses. The necessary supplies were already in the van. Due to the darkness and tinted windows, no one would notice anything which looked suspicious.*

*Several hours later, when most residents of the city were in bed, he had gone to the river. He had chosen the spot in advance and it was a good choice. The water was deep enough and the trees were in the right position.*

*Tantalus was a fitting point of reference for Peters. During the trial, he had felt tantalized by the judge...he kept offering hope, but just as a promising opportunity presented itself, the judge would find a way of causing it to be withdrawn.*

*After he returned from the river he was exhausted but felt peaceful. It had been a long night. Things were going even better than he had expected. He smiled as he tried to anticipate how police investigators would react to what they found. They, surely, had never seen anything like it.*

*It was too early to do much celebrating, since there was one more tormenter yet to silence. The celebrating would have to wait until the mission was fully accomplished.*

## **Twenty-Nine**

The time went fast from Thanksgiving until the end of the semester. Rebecca, Sarah and I continued to play pool with Dr Chambers on Wednesday nights. He had been quite pleased with our group project and told us privately it was the best of all that had been presented.

I had so many things keeping me busy that I didn't spend much time trying to resolve my romantic dilemma. That suited me fine. I was content to maintain the status quo for awhile longer. I had enough to worry about as I tried to successfully complete my first semester.

Psychology was giving me the most trouble. I didn't help my situation much by getting a C- on my term paper. That and my pathetic mid term would count for sixty percent of my grade. If the final was anything like the mid term, it was going to be hard to get a decent grade for the course.

I was feeling fairly comfortable with my other classes as finals approached.

There had been no new developments concerning Burt Atkins' planned trial and there were no announced leads concerning the murder of Clayton Brower. While I had been very interested in both cases earlier, I hadn't spent much time thinking about them. This was about to change.

On the Friday before finals week, the weather was cool and cloudy. Rebecca, Sarah and I went to the student center to have our lunch. As we walked by the TV, we noticed there was a breaking news story.

An anchorman from one of the local stations just started talking as we stopped to watch and listen.

"Earlier this morning, the body of Judge Franklin Peters of Atlanta was found by fishermen in the Chattahoochee River near the Pine Knoll River Park in Roswell," the anchorman said. "His body was suspended in an upright position by ropes tied to trees overhanging the riverbank. His upper body was above the water level, but his lower body was submerged. It appeared he had been murdered. Mrs. Peters had become concerned last evening when the Judge failed to come home to join her and some guests for dinner. When she hadn't heard from him for two hours, she had alerted police."

We looked at each other in shock, then turned back to the TV screen.

The anchorman continued, "As can be seen from our overhead helicopter, there is still much activity at the crime scene." While he was speaking we could see a close-up overhead shot which showed some boats in the river and some people on the riverbank. "We'll now go to our Jim Engle who is reporting from the scene."

"Thank you Vance. The judge's body was found by two fishermen at approximately eight fifteen this morning, about three hours ago, and they alerted police using a cell phone. A few minutes ago, I interviewed Junior Collins, one of the fishermen and here is a tape of that conversation."

"We were trolling slowly along the riverbank with our electric motor and were shocked when we came across a dead man tied to some trees and hanging in the river. We could tell he was dead just by looking at him and didn't try to do anything with him. We decided we shouldn't touch the body and called the police using 911 on my cell phone," Junior Collins said. "We waited for the police to get here and they asked us to stay here for awhile. They have questioned us some and want to see us again before we leave."

"Is the body still here?"

"No, they took it away a little while ago."

"How was the body tied to the trees?" Mr. Engle asked.

"There was a rope tied around his chest just under his arms. Another rope was strung through that rope and was tied to two trees hanging over the river bank."

"Did you see any people or suspicious activity around the body when you first saw it?"

"We didn't see any people, but we noticed some grapes hanging a few inches over the man's head."

"How deep was the water where the body was tied to the trees?"

"The river is often fairly shallow along the banks, but here it's pretty deep. His upper body was out of the water, but the water came almost up to his arm pits."

"Did you recognize the man when you found him?"

"No, but later we heard he was a judge from Atlanta named Peters,"

"Vance, that's what we learned from Junior Collins," Mr. Engle said. "The police haven't told us much yet, but did say the Judge had apparently been shot three times. We will remain on the scene hoping to get more information."

"Thanks, Jim," the anchorman replied. "We will keep following this story and will interrupt our normal programming to give important updates."

"I can't believe it," Sarah said with a drained look on her face. He was such a nice man. Elizabeth Peters will be devastated."

"This can't be," Rebecca exclaimed. "We just met him several days ago and now he's dead. That's hitting too close to home."

"Why would anyone hang him in a tree like that?" Sarah exclaimed. "It doesn't make sense."

"I know, it's so amazing," Rebecca said. "And, why would someone hang grapes above his head. It's all so bizarre. Hey, wasn't there some Greek myth about something like this? Ryan, didn't we read or talk in class about something?"

"I was thinking the same thing. It was in Costanza's class. What was the name of the man the gods punished in the Underworld by keeping water and food out of his reach?" I asked and then it came to me. "Now I remember. That was Tantalus. Every time he tried to drink or eat, the water or food was withdrawn."

"Do you think the murderer of Judge Peters was trying to simulate Tantalus?" Rebecca asked.

"Maybe," I said.

"That may be right," Sarah blurted. "But, why would someone do something like this? I still can't believe it."

"Maybe someone hated the judge so much because of one of his trials they decided to kill him," Rebecca responded.

"Could be," Sarah replied. "He may have made some enemies."

"I really liked him," Rebecca said. "I feel terrible about this."

"Me too," I added. "Are you guys thinking what I'm thinking about all of this?"

"What do you mean?" Sarah said.

"He's the third prominent person in Atlanta killed under strange circumstances in the last few months counting Mason and Brower," Rebecca answered.

"Not only strange," I said, "but, all of them seem tied into characters from Greece."

"Mason like Agamemnon, Brower like the suitors, and Peters like Tantalus," Rebecca concluded.

"Yeah," I said. "Did the same person or persons kill the three people or were there different murderers in each case?"

"Well, the police think Burt Atkins killed Mason," Sarah said. "If the same person killed all three people, that would mean Burt Atkins also killed Clayton Brower and Judge Peters. Does that seem likely to you?"

"Not to me," I said. "You'd think since he was facing trial in one murder case, he wouldn't put himself at further risk by going out and murdering two more people."

"Right," Rebecca said. "It wouldn't seem likely unless he had a very strong motive for doing so."

"Yes," Sarah said. "And, while he apparently had a motive for killing Dr. Mason, it's hard to see why he would have a motive for killing the other two men."

"I can't see what that motive would be," I added.

"If it isn't likely Burt Atkins killed the three men, do you think someone else killed all three of them?" Rebecca asked.

"We've all seen plenty about serial killers on TV and in the movies," Sarah replied. "And it seems serial killers usually follow certain patterns and/or leave certain clues. I think a serial killer killed all three men and, for some reason, he is following some pattern related to ancient Greece."

"We may be on target or we may be totally off base," I said.

"Yeah," Sarah replied. "I wonder if the police see any linkage between the three murders?"

We kept talking and sat down in the dining area after getting some food.

"Just to continue with our speculation," I said, "If we took the view that Burt Atkins was not guilty of any of the murders, who would have a motive for killing these three people?"

"That's a good question," Rebecca replied. "Judges, lawyers, and even doctors do things or make decisions which could create enemies."

"That's true," Sarah responded. "Could all three of them have made a common enemy?"

"That's possible," I said. "Perhaps it could have been due to something in their professional lives. Or, maybe there could have been some factor in their personal lives which would link them in the eyes of a common enemy."

"Like if they all had a common mistress or if they all had some incriminating information on the same person," Rebecca said.

"Right, or some other common element," I responded. "As intriguing as all of this is, we still have to concentrate on our finals. I don't feel I have the time to think about murders until I can put these tests behind me."

"Same here," Sarah replied.

## **Thirty**

On Sunday we found a vacant small conference room in the student center and met there to study for our Western civilization final. Sarah opened the conversation by saying, "My parents are still quite shaken up by Judge Peters' murder. They visited Elizabeth and feel she is holding up fairly well. Elizabeth has always worried that her husband was at some risk due to having spent so much time as a judge. She thinks some person, who may have been dismayed by one of the judge's decisions, could be responsible for his murder. She can't think of anything in particular, but doesn't know of any other reason why someone would have wanted to kill him."

"Did your mom of dad have any theories about who may have wanted to kill the judge?" I asked Sarah.

"Not really".

"Ryan, have you learned anything from Steve Simmons?" Rebecca asked.

"I spoke with him last night and learned some things which I haven't seen in the news yet. The judge's car was still in his assigned parking spot in a parking garage near the court house and the authorities feel someone abducted him on Friday afternoon around six p.m. when the judge was about to get into his car to go home after work. He left from his parking spot pretty consistently at that time every day, so a person familiar with his routine would know that would be a place where he could be captured. Three spent shell cartridges were found on the concrete floor near the driver's door to his car and the police think the judge was shot as he was about to get into his car. The gun probably had a silencer since nobody seems to have heard gunshots."

Sarah and Rebecca listened intently as I continued. "The police think the killer probably put the judge's body in a van or car trunk where it wouldn't be seen by the parking attendant when the killer left the garage. They think the killer took the body to the river later that evening. This all took place Thursday night and the body was found Friday morning by the fishermen."

"What a gruesome undertaking," Rebecca replied. "Sarah, have you heard anything from the coroner's office about this?"

"No, I haven't been working since this happened because they allowed me time off for my finals. If that's how it happened, that's awful."

"Steve was pretty familiar with the judge and some of the cases he had presided over during his long tenure on the bench," I said. "Steve said the police have no clues yet as to who the murderer may be."

"This is so terrible," Sarah said. "It's hard for me to understand how people get so angry that it leads to murder."

Our study session was successful. Somehow we were able to concentrate on our test and forget about the judge and other things. The next day we talked briefly after the test and felt we had been quite well prepared.

It was a hectic week. I didn't see Sarah the rest of the week and only saw Rebecca when we took our U.S. history test on Tuesday. By Thursday evening I was worn out and had only my psychology test left to take on Friday morning.

For some reason, I wasn't grasping the material in psychology very well and that bothered me. As I studied for the final, I couldn't stay awake and had to put my head down on the library table to sleep for awhile. That revived me somewhat, but I got drowsy again and had to sleep some more. When I was awake, I had trouble focusing on what I was trying to study and memorize. Finally, about midnight, I decided that any more effort would be futile so I went to my room and fell asleep immediately.

While I felt fairly rested when I sat down for the test the next morning at nine o'clock, I had a hard time with it. The multiple choice and true and false questions were confusing and I didn't have good answers for two of the short essay questions. All of this made me nervous and that didn't help a bit. I was one of the last students to finish and felt when I turned in my paper that pulling out a C for the course may be too much to hope for.

I plopped down on a bench on the mall to regroup and collect my thoughts. I was very glad to be done with all of my finals. What a relief after a pressure-filled week. It had been a real workout for me, but I felt I had done the best I could.

I felt more relaxed than I could ever remember. I got through it. If I got a D in psychology, so be it. I expected respectable grades in my other four classes.

I went back to my room and packed a bag before I started my long drive. Mike had already headed home and left me a note wishing me a Merry Christmas. I sent a brief e-mail to Rebecca and Sarah wishing them happy holidays and said I would see them when we all got back in January.

The trip home was a blur. I think my mind shut down after all the strain. While I had worried about getting sleepy, I stayed alert until I stopped at a small motel along the interstate about midnight. When I pulled into our driveway the next day, it struck me how nice it would be to see my parents and be home for the holidays, without having to crack a book for over two weeks.

There had been snow on the ground as soon as I had gotten through Chicago. I was hit with a blast of cold air as I opened my car door. "Welcome to Wisconsin," I said to myself as I walked up the sidewalk.

## **Thirty-One**

The first part of my holiday period was enjoyable, but it went by fast. My parents were glad to see me and I was glad to see them. The Christmas Eve service at our church was nice and, as was our custom, Mom, Dad and I opened gifts to each other after the service.

I saw several friends and went out with Monica twice. We were pleased to see each other. I could, however, tell that we had both been through many new experiences since we had gone off to school. I still felt close to her, but not as close as I had in August. Somehow, I sensed Monica may have been undergoing the same change in feelings that I was. I didn't think about things back in Atlanta much for the first several days, but then started getting a little anxious to get back. I got two short e-mails from Rebecca and one from Sarah. They were having nice holidays, but, like me, were looking forward to getting back to campus.

Then, three days before I was to drive back to Atlanta, a crisis arose. My mom had a heart attack and was rushed to the hospital. This was a big shock and the first couple of days were very tense. While Mom was still in serious condition in the hospital when it was time for me to leave, the doctors were showing more optimism than they had initially. Because of this, both Mom and Dad insisted it was not necessary for me to delay my return to campus.

I felt I shouldn't leave until she was better, but I reluctantly went back on schedule feeling she would be coming home soon.

*Alan Beske*

I got back to my dorm late and Mike was already asleep. I had worried about my mom's condition during my long drive and, while I was very tired, had trouble getting to sleep.

## **<u>Thirty-Two</u>**

Mike was gone when I woke up. I was feeling a little more optimistic about my mom but gave my dad a call to see how she was doing. I felt better after talking with him since her condition had improved a little.

On Monday, Wednesday and Friday I would have Greek mythology with Dr. Chambers, creative writing with Dr. Wilkens, and my continuing class in U.S. history with Dr. Costanza.

On Tuesday and Thursday, I would have anthropology and criminology. The course in criminology seemed especially appropriate now.

Rebecca and Sarah were already in the Greek mythology classroom when I arrived. I was glad to see them and said, "Morning guys. I missed you."

"Hi, Ryan," Rebecca said. "We were wondering when you'd show up. We missed you too."

"Hey Ryan," Sarah added. "We don't have our next class until one. What is your schedule?"

"My next one is at one too."

"Great," Rebecca said. "Let's have lunch after class and get caught up on we all did over the holidays."

Just then Dr. Chambers walked in and said enthusiastically, "Good morning everyone. I hope we are all in the proper room. This is Greek mythology and I'm Dr. Chambers."

"Sorry, but somehow I find I'm in the wrong place," a tall girl said sounding a little embarrassed as she got up and left the room.

"Good luck," Dr. Chambers said to her good naturedly as she left. "I'm glad to see so many familiar faces. He paused as he scanned the room and then said, "I'm especially pleased to see Charley, Diane, Jeff and Jerry. This is their third class with me. Then we have Ken and Rick who are seniors. This is their fourth class with me. I'd appreciate it if you'd all raise your hands." The six students raised their hands and smiled and Chambers continued, "They are all pretty sharp and can give those of you who don't know me some tips on how to prepare for my challenging tests."

As he was speaking I spotted Tyler and Laurel and waved at them.

"I assume you are all here since you have an interest in Greek mythology. It's certainly one of my favorite subjects and, by the time we end the semester, you'll understand, better than you do at present, the important role Greek mythology has played in our Western heritage."

By the time the session ended, Dr. Chambers had given an overview of what would be covered in the course and it seemed to me that most of the students were looking forward to our future sessions.

After class, we spoke briefly with Tyler and Laurel and then Rebecca, Sarah and I went to the student center for lunch.

"It looks like we'll be eating inside for awhile until it gets a little warmer," Sarah said.

"Yeah," Rebecca replied. "I guess we can handle that. Did you have nice holidays?"

"Pretty nice," Sarah said. "It was generally relaxing, although my parents are still feeling down because of Judge Peters' death."

"Have there been any new developments about the case reported in the media?" I asked.

"Not really," Sarah answered. "The police seem to have been conducting an aggressive investigation but no significant findings have been reported. I worked some at the coroner's office over the holidays and didn't learn anything there either."

"Rebecca, how was your holiday?" Sarah asked.

"I enjoyed seeing my parents and they are doing fine. I saw a few of my high school friends who were home from college and I spent some time relaxing on the internet. It was nice going home, but I'm glad to be back here."

"I feel the same," Sarah said. "It's strange. My home is less than thirty minutes from here, but I feel like I'm in a whole different world when I'm on campus." Sarah looked at me and said, "Ryan, how was your trip home?"

"The first part of my visit was great, but the last few days were not good."

"What happened?" Rebecca asked with a concerned look on her face.

"A few days before I came back, my mom had a heart attack. She was still in serious condition when I left home, but Mom and Dad insisted I return to school on schedule. This morning I called home and Dad said she's still in serious condition, but has improved some. I was really scared for awhile, but feel a little better now."

"I'm so sorry to hear about that," Rebecca said. "But, it's great to hear she's getting better."

"Ryan, that had to be very worrisome for all of you," Sarah added. "I wish your mom a speedy recovery."

"Thanks. When something like this happens, it really makes you think about the important things in life."

"Did you get a chance to see Monica when you were home?" Rebecca asked tentatively.

I could sense the concern in her voice and tried to answer carefully, "Yes. We went out a couple of times." She is doing fine and likes college so far." I left it at that since I was feeling confused about my feelings toward Monica and wanted to sound a little vague.

"That's nice," Rebecca answered, apparently not sure how to interpret my comments. Then, changing the subject she said, "Did you two get your grades?"

Sarah and Rebecca ended up with all A's and B's and I brought up the rear with four B's and a D in psychology. I wasn't surprised with their results since they were both so bright. Unfortunately, they had a good time ribbing me over my poor performance in psychology.

I had to rush to get to Dr. Wilkens' creative writing class but made it before she arrived. I recognized two students in the classroom. There were only about twenty of us and I liked the small class size.

Dr. Wilkens began the class by introducing herself and acknowledging me and a few other students whom she had had in prior classes. She reviewed the course content and her planned approach in her normal self-assured fashion and put us at ease with a few humorous comments. She looked terrific as usual and flashed a couple of smiles at me. That felt nice. I was glad to be taking another class from her.

After our U.S. history class Rebecca and I met with Dr. Costanza since he had more posters for us to distribute. If the start of the new year did anything to add warmth to his personality, it wasn't obvious to me.

Mike, David Brooks and five other guys from our hall were in my room when I arrived. I was glad to see everyone and joined in on the conversation. There was a lot of discussion about grades. After listening to how everyone did, I felt comfortable with my own results. I did a little better than average compared with those present. David said that Tom Warren and Jimmy Black had gotten poor grades and didn't come back for our new semester. Mike mentioned that two freshmen on the crew team had gotten poor grades and were quite nervous about their academic status.

## Thirty-Three

The next morning I called my dad to see how Mom was doing. The news was not as encouraging as I had hoped. He said that she was suffering from some complications but the doctors were hopeful she would react favorably to a new drug she had just been given.

Then, at nine o'clock, I attended my first anthropology class. Our professor was Dr. Victor Meyers. He was an obese man about sixty with red bushy hair. He looked like a circus clown without his costume and seemed to love an audience. I concluded that he'd keep us entertained in the weeks ahead.

My criminology class started at eleven. Sarah was there when I arrived. We felt comfortable with our professor, but our first class was uneventful.

Sarah and I had lunch together after class and then I worked in the library until about five o'clock. At that point I took a break and called Steve Simmons on my cell phone while standing on the front steps of the library.

Steve answered on the second ring.

"Steve, it's Ryan Anderson," I said. "I wanted to thank you for your help with my term paper on the Mason case. Dr. Wilkens liked my paper very much. How are you doing these days? Are you still following the Mason, Brower and Peters cases?"

"Ryan, it's good to hear from you," Steve replied. He sounded tense but was trying to be cordial. "I'm glad you did well on your paper. I'm still trying to follow all three cases, but there hasn't been much new news since before the holidays. Frankly this is turning into quite an ordeal for me and I'm not getting much sleep at night."

"I'm sorry to hear that." I said feeling a little concerned by the tone of his voice. "What's the problem?"

"I don't know for sure, but I feel my safety is being threatened," Steve replied cautiously. "Over the years, I've gotten some negative reactions from people who haven't liked certain things I've written about. It goes with the territory. However, this is different and it's really gotten me on edge."

"What is going on?" I asked feeling worried.

"This morning and the day before I found threatening notes tied to rocks on the front steps of my house. Some anonymous person must have put them there in the middle of the night. I found the notes when I went out to walk my dog before I went to work," Steve said guardedly.

"What did the notes say, if you don't mind my asking?" I asked hesitantly.

"The first one said, '**The sins of your past will soon be avenged.**' The one this morning said, '**Soon your public voice will be stilled forever and the citizens of Atlanta will be free of your brand of vile journalism,**'" Steve responded. "I don't know whether I'm the victim of a crazy practical joker or a person with serious intentions of doing me harm."

"Whoever is responsible, it seems like something you should be taking quite seriously."

"Yesterday I wasn't too alarmed. However, today, you can bet I'm taking it very seriously. I mentioned my concerns to my wife this morning and to a friend in the police department just before you called."

"That sounds like the right thing to do," I said reassuringly. "Please be very careful."

"I'll do that. Thanks for your concern. I do feel a little better having let the police know what was going on. They'll see if they can find who's behind this. Anyway, I'm about to get on a conference call, Ryan, and I need to run. I'll talk to you later."

"Bye, Steve, and good luck." This was the last time I ever spoke to him.

Around six o'clock the next day and I went to my room to watch the local news in case there were any new developments regarding the murder of Judge Peters.

While I learned nothing about the judge, the lead story was shocking. According to the anchor people, Steve Simmons' wife had reported him missing when he had failed to come home from work last night. He had called her about seven fifteen saying he was leaving the office to come home. That was the last she heard from him. When he didn't arrive home after a reasonable period of time, she had tried repeatedly to reach him on his cell phone, but had gotten no response. She got increasingly nervous since she was aware he had gotten some recent threatening messages and eventually called the police at about ten p.m. Simmons was last seen by co-workers when he left his office at approximately seven twenty p.m. His van was not found in the garage where he normally parked. He had not been heard from or seen by anyone since he left his office.

I was amazed at what was being reported. My phone conversation with Steve wasn't very long before he disappeared. I was extremely worried about what may have happened to him. I feared the worst and felt his disappearance surely must be due to some type of foul play.

It didn't take long before my worst fears were confirmed. I learned of some of the horrible details the next day as I watched the twelve o'clock news in the student center. Steve Simmons' body had been found a few hours earlier by workers in a quarry at the Marshall Marble Company located about sixty miles northeast of Atlanta. More details would be provided at a press briefing at five o'clock.

I was absolutely stunned and felt a strong need for some fresh air. I stumbled outside and plopped down on a bench on the mall. The sky was cloudy and the temperature was about fifty degrees, but the cool air helped clear my head. This was terrible. I had liked Steve and couldn't believe he was dead. The threats he had received were truly deadly. Why would someone kill him? Who would want to kill him? My mind was foggy and I couldn't think. I wanted to talk to someone and reached Rebecca on my cell phone and gave her the news. She was just as shocked as I was. We wanted to watch the five o'clock press briefing and agreed to meet in the student center a few minutes before it started.  Rebecca planned to contact Sarah to see if she could join us.

## **Thirty-Four**

*The Simmons matter was the most difficult of the four. There were more logistics involved and, while Simmons was well-restrained, it was a bit unnerving having him struggling behind the seat during the periods when he was conscious.*

*He had always considered Simmons to be arrogant, based on the words he used in his stories. He was anything but arrogant that night.*

*The only surprise was the flat tire he had to fix as he was about to pull out of the quarry. Fortunately, his spare was in good shape.*

*Later, he relaxed with a long hot shower. He let the steam build up. The water splashing against his skin seemed to wash his remaining tension away.*

*As he lay in bed, he felt fully relaxed for the first time in months. His plan was well-formulated. He had followed it perfectly. The results were exactly as he had hoped. While there had been numerous things which could have gone wrong, no problems had arisen. That was especially pleasing.*

*The tormentors had paid for their abuses. He felt satisfied, but he was not as exuberant as he expected he would be. This was a little unsettling, but he expected to have a greater level of satisfaction once some time separated him from the gruesome tasks he had performed.*

*Now, it was time to carry on with his life. He would close this chapter. He had gotten the necessary revenge. While he wasn't worried about being implicated in the murders, he knew he had to be vigilant to insure that his innocence was not threatened.*

## **Thirty-Five**

Rebecca, Sarah and I sat down by the TV set just before five. The briefing was conducted by Lieutenant Clarence Waters. In an opening statement he said that Steve had last been seen alive at approximately seven twenty p.m. on Thursday when he left his office. His body had been found by a worker in the quarry at approximately eight this morning, Saturday. A gag was in Steve's mouth, his hands were tied behind his back and his feet were bound together. His body was found in a sitting position with his back against a large block of marble. A long rope running under Steve's arms was used to tie him to the block. Death apparently resulted from three gunshot wounds to the chest. There were some surface wounds to his head and the letter "S" was scrawled on his forehead in blood.

Steve's van had been found Friday evening in a parking garage located two blocks from the parking garage where he normally parked for work. There were no suspects and a thorough investigation was in process. Lieutenant Waters fielded questions when he finished his opening statement.

A reporter in a brown leather jacket asked, "Have you determined if the victim was killed while tied to the block of marble or could he have been killed somewhere else?"

"Due to blood on the ground and bullet marks on the stone he was tied to, it appears he was shot after being tied to the stone," Lieutenant Waters responded.

"Has the time of death been determined?" asked a young woman with red hair.

"It appears that death occurred sometime Thursday evening. Based on wounds to the victim's head and blood stains in his van, it's appears that he may have been hit on the head and subdued when he was about to get in his van Thursday night after leaving his office. The assailant probably pushed the victim into the van where he was gagged and tied up so he couldn't move. Then, we're assuming the assailant drove to a nearby parking garage where the victim's van was left after the victim was transferred to another vehicle. From there, we believe the assailant drove the victim to the quarry where the victim was tied to the rock and killed."

A man with gray hair then asked, "Isn't it likely that someone may have seen such acts taking place?"

"If someone saw anything suspicious, we certainly hope they will come forward. The victim's vehicle was a camper van and, due to the curtains and tinted glass, it would have been hard for any observer to see anything in the back of the van. If the assailant had a van or put the victim in a car trunk, the victim could have been transported in the assailant's vehicle secretly."

"I have a question about the quarry," a well-dressed young man asked. "Would there have been anyone at the quarry who may have seen the assailant bring in the victim?"

"Guards are stationed at the entrance when workers are present during the daylight hours Monday through Saturday. At other times the front gate is locked and there are no guards on duty. Nobody would have been at the quarry on Thursday night. While the main gate would have been locked then, the assailant probably entered the property through a remote entrance which was open due to a broken gate."

Another reporter then asked, "If the victim was taken to the quarry and killed on Thursday night, wouldn't workers have seen his body some time on Friday?"

"There was no work done in that part of the quarry on Friday, but the body was discovered this morning when work resumed in that area."

An attractive woman in a black pants suit asked, "Do you have any explanation for the 'S' on the victim's forehead?"

"Not at this point," Lieutenant Waters replied curtly.

"Is it true that Mr. Simmons had gotten some threats before his murder?" a stocky man asked.

Lieutenant Waters looked surprised and agitated at the question and said. "Some of you reporters really did your homework. That's true, but I'm not prepared to elaborate on the nature of those threats at this time. I can only take two more questions."

The stocky man quickly asked, "Do you have any clues as to why the victim was killed in such a horrible fashion or who may have been responsible?"

"This is all very baffling at this point. We don't know why the victim was treated in such an unusual fashion, and we have not yet identified any suspects. Last question."

A tall man in a suit asked, "Do you think there may be any connection between this case and the murders of Dr. Peter Mason, Clayton Brower and Judge Franklin Peters? They were all prominent citizens and all were killed in unusual fashions."

"As you know, a person will soon stand trial for Dr. Mason's murder," Lieutenant Waters replied. "All avenues are still being explored. If there is any connection, we hope to find it. Thank you everyone. This is the end of our briefing."

"It's all so incredible," Sarah said. "What a terrible way to die."

"It really makes you wonder why a murderer would go through all of that to kill someone," Rebecca stated in awe. "Ryan, you knew him. This must be very upsetting to you."

"I feel terrible," I replied feeling very disturbed. "What makes it even more shocking is that I must have been one of the last people who talked with him. We had a phone conversation about five on Thursday afternoon and he was last seen when he left his office at seven-twenty."

Rebecca comforted me by putting her hand on my forearm and said, "Ryan, it's really is tragic. I'm so sorry it happened. Did Simmons say anything unusual in your phone conversation?"

"He did, and that makes me feel even worse," I replied on the verge of tears. "He mentioned he had received some threats and he seemed quite worried about his safety."

"What kind of threats?" Sarah asked as she pulled her chair closer to me and Rebecca.

I looked around briefly and saw there were no people close enough to us to hear our conversation and, speaking softly, explained what Steve had told me about the two threats. Rebecca leaned closer to me and put her warm hand on my forearm again, "Had Simmons told anyone about the notes?"

"Yes. After he got the second threat, he mentioned it to his wife and to someone in the police department."

"Did he have any idea who may have left him the notes?" Sarah asked.

"I don't think so."

"With all of the articles he had written over the years, I guess he must have upset a few people from time-to-time," Rebecca offered.

"I'm sure that's true," Sarah agreed. "Or, he may have done something else to have given someone a motive for murder."

"It sounds like he died a horrible death," Rebecca said in a strained voice.

"It's so gruesome and so bizarre," Sarah added. "Whoever killed him went to a lot of extra effort for some reason."

"The killer was obviously trying to make some kind of statement," Rebecca said. "He not only wanted to kill Simmons, but apparently wanted to symbolize something in the process."

"That's right," Sarah said. "It's like the murders of Dr. Mason, Clayton Brower and Judge Peters. In those cases, the people were not simply murdered, but the murderers did some grotesque things to the bodies, maybe some strange forms of symbolism."

"We had those first three strange murders of prominent citizens and now we have the murder of a fourth public figure," Rebecca said speculatively. "Like one reporter said, do you think all of these cases are linked in some way? Could some serial killer be responsible for all of this? It all reminds me of a movie where the murderer was replicating gruesome killings which had been carried out by a murderer in an old mystery book."

"I'll bet something similar is happening here," Sarah said. "Not that the killer is following a mystery book, but he's following some kind of pattern."

"I think you're on the right track," I responded. "I wouldn't be surprised if one person killed all of them and that person is on some kind of mission seeking revenge for some reason."

"We talked about these things after Judge Peters was killed and concluded Burt Atkins didn't seem like a serial killer," Rebecca said. "Now there are four murders. I really don't think he's guilty of any of them especially now that we're seeing an even broader picture."

"Not unless he was crazy and didn't care about the consequences," Sarah added. "He had a possible motive in the case of Mason, but he doesn't have obvious motives in the other cases."

"Everything seems to say a serial killer is involved, and it's not Burt Atkins. There are similarities between all four of the murders," I said, trying to summarize. "In each case, the murderer not only killed the victims, but went out of his way to do some very unusual things which must symbolize something. Secondly, each of the victims was a person of some prominence in Atlanta. That's very unusual. While murders happen from time-to-time, they usually happen to non-prominent people in drug-related, domestic violence or road rage type incidents. Thirdly, the murders happened within a few months of each other. Lastly, in the case of the first three at least, there seems to be some type of connection with ancient Greece."

"Good points," Sarah said with interest. "Do you see any Greek connection in the Simmons murder?"

"That's what I've been trying to think about while the shock of his murder has been sinking in," I answered. "Everything has been happening so fast, I haven't had a chance to think. There's a thought in the back of my mind that's nagging at me, but I can't focus on it."

"You said Steve found threatening notes tied to rocks on his front steps," Rebecca said. "The notes must have been left by the killer. He was also tied to a rock and was killed in a rock quarry. It's as if the killer was foretelling how Steve would die. Maybe the rocks even came from the quarry where he was killed."

"Maybe," Sarah said. "So, let's say the notes tied to the rocks were symbolic. Then, the 'S' scrawled in blood on Steve's forehead must also be symbolic."

"Probably," Rebecca said. "He was gagged and his hands were tied. The threatening notes had talked about ending his style of vile journalism. Tied hands and a gagged mouth could symbolize that a person had been stopped from communicating."

"That right," Sarah said in agreement.

"Lieutenant Waters said Steve was found in a sitting position with his back against a large block of marble and he was tied to the marble. That reminds me of something, but I can't recall what. Wait a minute!" I blurted out having an inspiration. "Rebecca, do you have your Greek mythology book in your backpack?"

"Yes," Rebecca replied as she removed it from her bag and handed it to me.

I quickly started flipping through the pictures in the center of the book. I had looked at these a couple of times previously when I had started reading the book. "This is what I was trying to remember. Sisyphus!" I said excitedly. "Do you remember who he was? He was the person who offended Zeus and tricked Pluto and was punished by having to spend eternity in the Underworld trying to roll a huge boulder up a hill. However, each time he got it nearly to the top of the hill it rolled back and he had to start all over again. Look at this picture!" I exclaimed as I held the open book for Rebecca and Sarah to see. The artist had depicted Sisyphus leaning his back into a huge boulder straining to roll it up a hill. His arms were stretched behind him steadying the rock as he pushed it with his back and he was pushing so hard that he was almost in a sitting position.

"I remember that story now," Sarah said staring at the picture.

"I do too," Rebecca added. "We talked about it in Costanza's class. When Steve was tied against the block of marble with his hands tied behind his back, he probably did look something like this."

"Yes," Sarah said. "And the 'S' on his forehead must stand for Sisyphus!" Sarah exclaimed.

"I think you are both right on target," I said excitedly. "The killer must have, for some reason, been representing Sisyphus when he killed Steve."

"Are you thinking what I'm thinking?" Rebecca said raising her voice.

"I think so," Sarah blurted out. "This makes the fourth murder that seems to be related to ancient Greece."

"Right," I said eagerly. "Mason was murdered like Agamemnon; Brower was murdered like the suitors; the judge's body was displayed like Tantalus; and Steve Simmons's death related to Sisyphus."

"What's common between those four Greek characters?" Sarah asked.

"They were all punished for something they had done," I replied.

"If the killer patterned the murders after these ancient Greek men who were punished for offenses, then the killer maybe was punishing our four victims for some offenses which the killer felt had occurred against himself or others," Sarah said.

"Yeah," Rebecca added. "If that were true, what could the victims have done that would have offended or harmed someone? If we knew that, maybe it would offer clues as to who the killer was."

"Maybe the killer isn't done yet," I speculated. "Perhaps he has more murders planned."

"Wouldn't that be awful," Rebecca said. "Four people have been killed already. Hopefully there won't be others."

"Just think. Things have started to hit closer to home, so to speak," I said. "Sarah's parents knew Dr. Mason and Judge Peters; Sarah's dad knew Clayton Brower; we all knew Judge Peters; and I knew Steve Simmons. If there were any more murders, would we know those victims also?"

"When you put it that way, it sounds pretty scary," Rebecca said sounding concerned.

"Ryan's right," Sarah added. "This is all pretty unsettling."

"I got intrigued with the first three murders, but Steve's murder has really shaken me up," I said seriously. "I'm worried that the murderer isn't done yet and I'm worried about who the next victim might be. I think we should do what we can to support the police in solving these cases."

"I agree," Sarah said.

"Absolutely" Rebecca said agreeing. "There must be some things we could do to help. I'm starting to feel a little like Sherlock Holmes already."

"Okay," I said. "We're agreed that we'll do some work on this. I'm not sure the police would want any help from a few college kids, but I feel we should at least try to meet with the proper authorities and explain our theory about the linkage with ancient Greek personalities."

"That sounds like a good idea," Sarah said. "The question is, which authorities do we see since different jurisdictions are involved. The Mason and Simmons cases are probably being handled by the counties north of the metro area where the bodies were found. The

Brower case is being handled by Atlanta people. Judge Peters was apparently shot in Atlanta, but his body was found in the river outside the city limits, so I'm not sure who's handling that case."

"It sounds a little complicated," Rebecca responded.

"Yeah, but that shouldn't hold us back," I said. "Why don't we start with Lieutenant Waters, the guy who's handling the Simmons case. I feel personally connected to that one."

## **Thirty-Six**

After a few phone calls and some pleading on my part, I finally got through to Lieutenant Waters about ten p.m. At first he tried to put me off, but I eventually was able to set an appointment at his office for four o'clock Sunday afternoon.

Lieutenant Waters met us when we arrived and ushered us into a small conference room. Two of his associates were already in the room. They were Lieutenant Grimes and Sergeant Henderson. We all introduced ourselves and then Lieutenant Waters said impatiently, "Okay, Ryan, you explained on the phone why you wanted to meet with us. Please repeat and expand upon what you want to tell us. I don't know if it's important or not, but let's hear what you have to say. Sarah and Rebecca, speak up if you have anything to add."

He was quite abrupt and the three of us seemed really out of our element amongst these three burly detectives. I was immediately nervous, but swallowed hard to get my composure and then spent several minutes, without interruption, explaining how each of the four murders related to ancient Greek myths and legends. At first the officers looked disinterested as if they expected this meeting to be a waste of time. However, by the time I had finished my comments, they all had become attentive.

Lieutenant Waters then asked, "Do you girls concur with what he just said?"

Both girls nodded and then he turned back to me and said, "So, Ryan, is it your feeling the four murders were probably committed by the same person, a serial killer, and that the person is other than Burt Atkins, the person waiting to stand trial for murder of Dr. Mason?"

"That's correct," I replied. "Granted it's a theory, but it's logical that the same person was involved. In terms of Burt Atkins, it seems unlikely he would commit three murders while awaiting trial for the murder he's been accused of."

"If you're correct, Ryan," Lieutenant Waters said with a sharp tone in his voice, "you're contending the wrong person has been charged with the murder of Dr. Mason."

I knew that question would arise and it made me a little uncomfortable now that it had actually been raised. Nevertheless, I tried to answer diplomatically when I said, "I understand that and obviously am not privy to all of the evidence which has been considered in the case of Mr. Atkins. As I said, I have presented what seems to be a logical theory for your consideration concerning the four murders. We felt is was our duty to make you aware of our thoughts, not only in case this would be helpful in solving any of the murders, but, probably more importantly, we wanted to help prevent any possible future related murders," I said catching my breath. "Perhaps this theory is wrong, but we think it should be considered. Maybe Burt Atkins was involved or maybe not. We don't think he was."

"Okay, Ryan," Lieutenant Waters responded sounding a little conciliatory, "I think everyone knows we are faced with four very unusual killings. Please rest assured that all of the officers working on these cases are trying diligently to solve them as fast as possible. And, we are certainly open to ideas and information which can be helpful. As it now stands, Burt Atkins seems to be the person who killed Dr. Mason. Of course, a jury will be determining if he is judged guilty or not." He then stood up and said, "Anyway, thanks to all three of you for coming in today and giving us your thoughts. We will take your information under consideration along with everything else that will be considered. That's as far as we can go today. If you become aware of any additional information which you feel would be of importance to us, please give one of us a call. Of course, our team is only working on the Simmons case. Other jurisdictions are investigating the other three murders you discussed. However, we have been coordinating, and will continue to coordinate, with them as appropriate."

Everyone else stood up and we thanked Lieutenant Waters and his associates for meeting with us. They gave us their business cards as we left.

On the ride back to campus Rebecca said, "Ryan, you handled that very well. Good job."

"Yeah, Ryan," Sarah added, "They were a little intimidating at first, but you maintained your cool and got their attention."

"Thanks. We did the right thing."

By time we got back to Chancellor, we had resolved to get actively involved in trying to find clues which would help the police solve the murders.

As I sat in the library after eating with Mike and two other guys from my hall, I reflected on my challenges for the semester. I was going to have a lot of reading and would have to write a total of six papers. While I was having a good time with the band, that would continue taking a lot of my time. Furthermore, any time we spent trying to help solve the murders would create more pressures. I'd just have to make the most of it.

My pager vibrated and brought me out of these musings. My home phone number was on the small screen. I immediately got concerned. This was the first time my parents had paged me since I came to Chancellor and the apparent sense of urgency made me nervous.

I quickly went out to the front steps of the library and called home on my cell phone. It was about ten p.m. and Dad answered on the first ring. We had spoken regularly as my mom remained in the hospital in stable condition. He explained Mom's condition had worsened due to a respiratory infection. A new specialist was being called in. Hopefully, he could be of help. Dad said he would page me if there were any changes.

## **Thirty-Seven**

I got to Dr. Chambers class at the last minute the next morning. I had slept poorly due to worrying about my mom. I smiled weakly at Rebecca and Sarah as Dr. Chambers began speaking. He surprised me when he asked if any of us had heard about the murder of Steve Simmons. Most of the students raised their hands. Rebecca, Sarah and I shared glances and I think they were as curious as I was as to why Dr. Chambers had raised the question.

Dr. Chambers then said, "This murder may have some relationship to our class and I think we should discuss it. What do you remember about any details reported in the media concerning how the body was found? I'm going to make some notes on the board as we talk."

Laurel was the first person to respond and she said, "The victim was found in a stone quarry."

Dr. Chambers wrote "stone quarry" on the board.

Tyler then said, "The victim's back was tied to a block of marble."

Other students spoke up and Dr. Chambers made notations on the board after each comment. The list soon looked like this:

"stone quarry"
"back tied to marble block"
"hands tied behind back"
"shots to chest"
"S on forehead"
"gag in mouth"

"Have any of you looked ahead at the pictures in the middle of our textbook?" Dr. Chambers asked. "Does this list remind you of any of those pictures?"

There was a scramble and the sound of zippers zipping as most students retrieved their textbooks from their backpacks and began flipping through the pages. Rebecca, Sarah and I glanced at each other as we listened to the pages turning. After about a minute, someone called out, "Look at Sisyphus on page two-eleven. He's shown with his back against the huge bolder which he is trying to roll up a hill. Simmons' back was against a large block of stone, like a bolder. Also, the 'S' on his forehead could stand for Sisyphus."

I could hear everyone flipping through their books to find that picture, which was already imprinted in my mind. A girl in the back of the room said, "I think he's right." And a boy near the door said, "Of the characters pictured in our book, 'Sisyphus' seems like the right answer."

"That's also what came to my mind," Dr. Chambers replied. "We will be discussing Sisyphus in some depth later in the course and many of you, undoubtedly, have heard of him since he is one of the better known personalities in Greek mythology."

Laurel and Tyler joined Rebecca, Sarah and me for lunch after class and we spent some time talking about our classroom discussion about the parallel between Steve's death and Sisyphus. We also explained to Laurel and Tyler the parallels we saw between the other three murders and Greek characters and how this had led us to discuss our ideas with the police.

After Laurel and Tyler left, Sarah said, "We decided yesterday we would think about things we could do to help the police solve these crimes. Any ideas?"

"I'm going to do some internet research and see if I can come up with anything of interest," Rebecca answered.

"Good," Sarah said. "We visited the Appalachian Trail in the case of Dr. Mason and we went by Clayton Brower's house. Maybe we should visit the river and stone quarry sites where Judge Peters and Steve Simmons were found."

"That seems logical," I said.

"What if we try to talk with the wives of the four victims to see if we can learn anything from them?" Sarah proposed.

"It's a little delicate, perhaps, but it's worth a try," Rebecca replied. "Is there anything you can learn at the coroner's office, Sarah?"

"Possibly. I'll give it a try."

"Maybe we could try to find out if there were any warnings in advance given to Mason, Brower and Peters as happened with Simmons," I said.

"That's a good point," Sarah said. "Now we just need some time to do these things."

## **Thirty-Eight**

On Wednesday night, Rebecca, Sarah and I sat and talked with Dr. Chambers a few minutes before playing pool. We talked about our recent class discussion on the Sisyphus-Simmons connection. We then told Chambers that we had met with the police to explain how all four of the murders seemed to relate to Greek myths and how we gave them our theory that a serial killer was behind all of the murders.

Dr. Chambers had been listening intently with a strange look on his face as we talked and then he said in a strained voice, "You really must be taking this seriously to have gone to the police. What was their reaction, if you don't mind my asking?"

"They took in what we had to say, but we didn't get much of a reaction from them," Sarah said.

"Someone will soon stand trial for the Mason murder," Dr. Chambers said, leaning toward the center of the table as he spoke. He had a distant look in his eye. "Given that, what did they think about your theory of there being one killer behind all four of the murders?"

"We're not sure," I responded. "They apparently feel the proper person has been charged with that crime, but said things were now in the hands of the jury."

"Did they seem concerned that more murders could take place in the future?" Dr. Chambers asked.

"They didn't really say much about that," Rebecca said.

"Well, I think you did the right thing in sharing your ideas with the police," Dr. Chambers said cautiously, without much conviction. "You showed good initiative."

"It may not help much, but we're glad we met with them," I said. "We also plan to look for any other information which would be helpful to the police. We may not come up with anything, but want to put some effort into it. If we learned anything which would prevent a future murder, it would be worth it."

"That's true," Dr. Chambers said. "You said you were drawn to these cases due to your familiarity with the victims. I find myself in the same position. I believe I already mentioned to you that I was familiar with Dr. Mason and Clayton Brower since they were involved in the malpractice trial after my wife's death. That at first just seemed coincidental, but it's only part of the story." He paused and shifted his glance around the table to each of our faces and then continued. "Now, I'm really intrigued. You see, the judge in that case was Franklin Peters and Steve Simmons covered the trial for the *Atlanta Herald.*"

"That's amazing," Sarah said.

"Yes it is, and, like the three of you, I have gotten very caught up in these cases," Dr. Chambers continued intently. Then his mood shifted abruptly and he, attempting to sound cheerful, said, "This is all too depressing. You came here to play pool didn't you? Sarah and I will challenge Ryan and Rebecca. What do you say?"

We played until about eight when Dr. Chambers left after saying he wasn't feeling well. He had seemed frustrated and distracted and unexpectedly missed some easy shots.

The rest of us stayed and talked for awhile.

"I'm feeling a little uneasy," Sarah said with a troubled look. "Am I the only one?"

"Are you talking about Dr. Chambers?" Rebecca replied. "He seemed strange tonight if that's what you mean?"

"More than strange," I said cautiously. "He's normally so upbeat, but he seemed like a different person when we were talking about the murders and our meeting with the police. Something was bothering him and it clearly affected his pool game."

"He was definitely not his normal self tonight," Sarah said. "Maybe the linkage of the four murder victims with his wife's trial brought back sad memories. But, maybe there is another explanation," She lowered her voice and glanced around our table to make sure no one was nearby. Then leaning toward the center of the table she said, "I'm hesitant to say this, but I'm wondering if he may have had something to do with the murders. He could have a possible motive. We don't know any details, but perhaps he blamed those men for his unsuccessful malpractice trial and decided to get revenge."

"Oh my gosh!" Rebecca exclaimed in a loud whisper. "What if you're right?"

"It's not a comfortable thought, but she may be right," I said quietly. "We already know how he feels about Mason and Brower. Maybe he was upset with Judge Peters' handling of the trial."

"You're making sense, Ryan," Rebecca said softly. "So, Dr. Chambers could have had a grudge against three of the victims. That leaves Simmons. He could have also had a grudge against Simmons if he was upset with the way Simmons reported on the trial."

"I'm shocked we're talking this way," Sarah added. "We've admired Chambers and have become quite close to him. It's hard to believe he would ever murder anyone. Yet, it's possible there is a sinister side of him below the surface."

"I also find it hard to believe he would ever get upset to the point where he would murder someone," Rebecca said. "However, it's certainly intriguing that all four of the victims were linked to the malpractice trial. Also, Chambers is an expert on ancient Greece and it seems to me the killer or killers must know something about Greece to have committed the crimes the way they did."

"Maybe that's just a coincidence, but it may mean something," I added.

"This is all very sobering," Sarah said. "I feel like I've just been run over by a truck. What do we do now, if anything?"

"Maybe Chambers is the guilty party, or maybe it's someone else," I said. "Regardless, I think we need to keep investigating as we had planned."

"Ryan's right," Rebecca said. "And we need to first focus our investigations carefully on Dr. Chambers. For one thing, I'm going to see what I can find out about the malpractice trial on the internet."

"That's a good idea," Sarah said. "Could you also find out anything useful about Dr. Chambers through the library computer system?"

"Good point, I'll look into that," Rebecca said. Then she looked at Sarah and said, "Sarah, you may not like this idea, but hear me out.

Chambers seems quite infatuated with you. He would invite you on a date in a heartbeat if you ever gave him any encouragement. What if you went on a couple of exploratory dates with him to see if he might let his guard down and give you any clues which would clarify his guilt or innocence?"

Sarah stared at Rebecca, thinking, and looked at me. Then she said, "Why not? It's worth a try. Since we're getting devious, what if I got him occupied some evening and the two of you used that opportunity to search his office for possible useful clues?"

"I'm surprised at both of you," I said. "However, I like both of those ideas. I guess we all have to takes some risks in life, and this is for a good cause."

"Ok, we have an initial game plan concerning Chambers," Sarah said with a sly smile. "I'm feeling a little wicked, but, the hell with it. I'll keep thinking about our strategy and let you know what I come up with."

"Whatever we do regarding Chambers, I think it's important we keep this between the three of us and not do anything to tip him off concerning our suspicions about him."

## **Thirty-Nine**

*He actually liked Ryan, Rebecca and Sarah. They were sharp and pleasant to be with. But, they were now becoming a threat. He couldn't take any chances. They were expendable if it came to that.*

*He didn't really want to kill them and hoped he could prevent that by discouraging them from any more amateur detective work and police involvement.*

*First he would try to threaten Ryan, not too severely initially. This could be intensified. Threats to his two lovely friends could come later if required.*

# **Forty**

Thursday afternoon and evening, despite my concerns about my mom, Dr. Chambers and the murders, I was successful in getting reasonably caught up in my studies. In order to keep my momentum going, I didn't take any time to relax with Sarah after our criminology class. I was exhausted when I finally went to bed, but had trouble falling asleep. My mind kept wandering and I was tense. I'd fall asleep, but slept lightly and kept waking up.

The door from our dorm room to the hall had a one inch gap between the bottom of the door and the floor, and, while the lights in the hallways were dimmed from midnight to six a.m., I could always see a band of light under the door from my bed.

During one my periods of semi-consciousness, I heard a faint sound near the door. At first I thought I was dreaming, but then realized I was partially awake. My head had been turned to the wall and I slowly rotated it and looked toward the door. There appeared to be something on the floor just inside the door. The light was dim and my eyes were blurry, but it looked like an envelope.

I glanced at the illuminated digital face of my alarm clock and saw it was almost three thirty. My mind started to race and I was startled into full wakefulness. Why would anyone put an envelope under our door in the middle of the night? Mike was breathing softly and was oblivious to what had happened. Many students had unusual sleeping patterns and there were often people in the hallways at all hours of the night. Maybe one of our friends decided to leave us a note after a late night study session. That was the logical explanation.

Since I was trying hard to get some sleep, I didn't get up and look at the envelope, feeling it might be harder to fall asleep after getting up. As I started to doze off, I began to speculate about the envelope and again became wide awake. I kept thinking about the envelope and finally decided to get up and see what it contained. If it was for Mike I'd leave it for him. If it was for me, I'd open it.

I shuffled quietly to the door and knelt down. With the light coming under the door, I could see **"RYAN ANDERSON"** printed on the envelope in large bold capital letters. Since turning on a light might awaken Mike, I lay on my stomach on the cold tile floor hoping to read any message with the light from the hallway. The temperature shock to my bare skin caused me to recoil and made me tense. I opened the envelope as noiselessly as possible. It contained a sheet of typing paper which I unfolded and flattened against the floor by the bottom of the door.

I could read the message clearly and immediately felt my heart racing and my muscles contracting. It was typed in large bold capital letters and read: **"DON'T BECOME ANOTHER VICTIM LIKE SIMMONS."**

My head was spinning. After a few moments, I struggled to my feet and quietly slipped the note and envelope into my backpack, gritting my teeth trying to suppress the sound of the nylon zipper, and slid back into bed. My stomach still felt numb from the cold floor. I could hear Mike's soft breathing and was relieved that he hadn't woken up. For some reason, I felt it would be best not to tell him anything about what had happened. Not now. Maybe later. I tried to get a grip on myself, but was sick with anxiety. Even with my eyes closed I could picture the words of the note.

It was clearly meant for me. The envelope had my name on it. What did it mean? Who had delivered it? It had to relate to the murders because of what the note said. Had it come from the murderer or was it just a practical joke from someone? There were some practical jokesters on our hall, two of whom happened to be in my Greek mythology class. Maybe one of them had something to do with this. I knew that some other people on our hall had found anonymous notes in their rooms or in their backpacks. It could just be somebody's idea of a sick joke. But, maybe the note was from the murderer.

While we weren't sure, we thought Dr. Chambers could be the murderer. He or anyone else would have been able to get into the dorm. Student and faculty addresses, phone numbers and e-mail addresses were found in the electronic campus directory, so my room number was no secret. It took a programmed ID card to open the exterior doors to the dorms, but people routinely walked in behind residents when they opened the doors. Even Rebecca or Sarah could have left the note as a joke, but that didn't seem likely. I had trouble calming down, but eventually fell asleep.

I had no appetite in the morning and skipped breakfast.

I couldn't concentrate during Dr. Chambers' class. On the surface, everything seemed normal. He was conducting the class in his usual confident and cheerful fashion. I kept wondering if we were right in suspecting him as the murderer. The sooner we could find an answer to that question, the better.

After class, Rebecca, Sarah and I found a table in the student center and started having our lunch. They listened intently as I told them about the note and showed it to them. They could tell I was worried. I asked if they had anything to do with it and it was clear they knew nothing about it.

"As you said, Ryan, it could be a practical joke," Rebecca said, trying to put me at ease.

"True," I replied. "I don't know what to think, but want to get to the bottom of it as fast as I can to get rid of the anxiety it's giving me."

"The note is making me nervous too," Sarah said in a comforting voice. "Rebecca, have you found out anything yet with your computer?"

"Yeah," Rebecca said quietly. "I found a few articles which Steve Simmons had written about the malpractice trial related to the death of Chambers' wife. As we knew, Dr. Mason had been charged with malpractice and Dr. Chambers had been represented by Clayton Brower. Judge Peters was the presiding judge. There were expert witnesses presented by both sides. It sounded like much hinged on the testimony of one of the expert witnesses for the defense. There was a lot of debate concerning whether or not he should be allowed to testify. The judge wasn't convinced by Brower's arguments to block the testimony and ruled that the witness could be heard. It appears Dr. Chambers probably lost the case because of what that witness had to say."

Rebecca paused and continued, "After the trial, Chambers was quoted as being very upset with Clayton Brower and Judge Peters."

"None of that is surprising, I guess," Sarah said. "Could you tell why Chambers may have been upset with how Simmons reported the case?"

"Good question," Rebecca answered. "It's a little hard to say without having been a part of the trial, but there was a cynical flavor to Simmons' words which might not have been appreciated by Dr. Chambers."

"Rebecca," I said. "From the articles, does it seem Dr. Chambers could have been upset enough with Mason, Brower, Peters and Simmons to eventually murder all four of them?"

"Possibly"

"Good detective work, Rebecca," Sarah said. "Did you find anything else?"

"I checked the library borrowing records on both Dr. Chambers and Dr. Costanza and didn't find anything there," Rebecca replied. "I decided to check on Costanza while I was checking up on Chambers. While we haven't talked much about Costanza, he's always seemed a little weird and threatening to me and he had some discussion about Agamemnon, Sisyphus, and Tantalus last semester."

"Yeah, and Costanza knows a lot about ancient Greece," I added. "He could be a possible suspect if he had motives."

"Just keep listening," Rebecca said excitedly, almost whispering. "I found both Chambers and Costanza have had some papers and books published. Most of these didn't catch my eye, but I noticed that Costanza published two papers in history journals related to murders and other forms of violence in ancient Greece."

"How interesting," Sarah replied. "I wonder if that means anything important."

"Maybe yes and maybe no," I said. "It's another reason to think of him as a possible suspect, but he doesn't seem to have obvious motives like Dr. Chambers."

"I agree," Sarah said. "Rebecca, you've come up with some good information."

"Thanks. Sarah, have you learned anything at the coroner's office about any of these cases that we're not aware of?"

"No. Brower was the only one in our jurisdiction and I haven't learned anything new on him. But, I'm ready to see what I can learn by going into my seductress role," Sarah said with a devilish grin.

"Oh yeah," Rebecca said, "The good doctor won't stand a chance when you go into action."

Sarah looked at both of us and replied smiling, "I think I can handle this role alright."

"Heaven help him," I said.

"Okay, Cleopatra," Rebecca said, "Please tell us your plan of attack."

"Of course," Sarah replied checking to make sure no bystanders could hear her. "While it's serious business any time you're dealing with a probable murderer, somehow, I'm looking forward to the challenge, dangerous as it may be."

"Whatever you do, you must be very careful," I said.

"Right," Sarah said and continued. "Anyway, here's what I've been thinking about. We'll join Dr. Chambers on Wednesday night as usual for pool. The two of you will find an excuse to leave early and I'll use my charms to keep him occupied while you sneak into his office and hunt around for any clues which may implicate him in the murders. Now that we have some reason to suspect Dr. Costanza, you should also search his office while you're at it. Actually, you could each do an office at the same time or one of you could act as a lookout while the other was in the offices. That's for you to figure out."

"This is getting interesting," Rebecca said. "Ryan and I can handle that."

"While you two are out doing your detective work, I'll start subtly trying to get the professor more interested in me as a date prospect. I'll see if I can get him to relax in hopes that I can, without being suspicious, get him to reveal anything about the malpractice trial or other matters which would help establish his guilt in the murders. Also, I'll get on the subject of home cooking and see if he'll invite me to his home or apartment for dinner. If he goes for that, while I'm there I'll look around for clues as best I can, but mainly I'll make some observations which will help the two of you break into his place to look for clues later when I have him occupied at a movie or something."

"Sarah, you devil, you," I said.

Sarah looked at me with an enigmatic smile and said, "Ryan dear, you're right about that. I'm not always the prim and proper Southern girl you've come to know and love. If the circumstances call for it, I can show a little flexibility."

I was surprised to be hearing some of the things Sarah was saying. There was definitely another side of her which wasn't apparent to the casual observer. I was finding this intriguing. She really was a girl with many talents.

"Okay, I get the point," I said "The stakes are high and this calls for special behavior. Count me in. I'll do my part to help solve these crimes. I just don't want any of us to get hurt."

"Nor do I," Sarah replied soothingly.

"Cool plan" Rebecca said. "What else have you come up with?"

"That's all so far. Let's do these things first and then see what that yields. In the meantime, we can hold off on the other things we were going to investigate. Are you with me in this?"

Rebecca and I both nodded and Rebecca said, "You've come up with a good plan. Are you saying you would go to bed with Chambers?" Rebecca asked cautiously.

Sarah got serious, looked at Rebecca and then me, and replied, "I really don't want things to go that far. I want to get him interested in me for the reasons mentioned, but need to be very careful about how much encouragement I give him. Don't let my outward confidence fool you. I'm nervous as hell about all of this, but feel it must be done."

"Ryan," Rebecca said. "You and I need to figure out how we're going to get into those two offices and do so without getting caught."

"Right," I replied. "Sarah, suppose that we have an excuse for leaving you and Chambers at eight o'clock on Wednesday night? Does that sound about right?"

"That sounds fine."

"Good," I said. "Rebecca, why don't we case the joint a couple of nights in order to plan our strategy around janitors or other people? Also, if we find the office doors to be locked, we'll need a way to get them open."

"Good idea. In terms of the doors, I may be able to help."

I wondered what she meant by that statement, but decided not to ask for clarification.

"I'll let you two worry about the offices," Sarah said. Rebecca's and my hands were resting on the table. Sarah reached out and placed her hands on ours and said as she squeezed, "We're all in this together. We can do this. We must do this. Agreed?"

"Absolutely," I said.

"Absolutely," Rebecca echoed.

## **Forty-One**

Monday night Rebecca and I went to the History Department at eight o'clock. We first walked through the whole department and found no one there. The lights were on and the doors to individual offices were closed. I noticed that a waste basket in the reception area was full and assumed the cleaning people hadn't been through the department yet.

There was only one entrance to the department. I stood as a lookout in the area outside the department and pretended to be looking at a bulletin board while Rebecca went back by the offices. The sound of a vacuum cleaner was coming from the Sociology Department which shared the foyer by the elevator with the History Department. The elevator opened and a cleaning woman, without paying any attention to me, rolled her cart from the elevator into the Sociology Department. The vacuum cleaner stopped, I heard some muffled voices, and then it started again.

Shortly after that, Rebecca came out to the foyer, winked at me, and we got on the elevator. We didn't talk until we took an isolated quiet table in the student center.

"Any luck?" I asked.

"We should be fine. All of the doors to the professors' offices, including Chambers' and Costanza's, were locked. Interestingly enough, my student ID card, when slipped between the door and the jam, serves as a good makeshift key if it's used properly. I was able to open both of the target offices. The waste baskets had papers in them. Maybe the cleaning people will come through and empty them later or maybe the professors empty their own baskets when they feel like it."

"Aren't you clever. Your many talents continue to amaze me."

"One of my ex-boyfriends taught me some useful things. Did you see anything interesting?"

"While I was standing guard, the cleaning people were working in the Sociology Department next door. I wouldn't be surprised if they go to the History Department next."

"You may be right. Why don't we go over there again tomorrow night a little after eight and hang around to see if that's what happens?"

"Good idea."

We got to the History Department at ten minutes after eight on Tuesday night. Someone was running a vacuum cleaner in the Sociology Department. We pretended to be looking at the bulletin boards and other displays in the foyer and probably didn't look suspicious.

At approximately eight twenty-five, two cleaning workers, one man and one woman, came out of the Sociology Department, each pushing a cart. We didn't pay any attention to them as they pushed their carts across the foyer and into the History Department. We moved closer to the door and listened.

"I'll get the trash out of the offices if you'll vacuum the carpet in the reception area and hall. Okay?" the man said. "We can vacuum in the offices next week."

"Okay by me," the woman replied.

We then heard the sound of a key unlocking a door and a vacuum starting. I motioned to Rebecca. We left quietly and got on the elevator.

We debriefed back in the student center.

"I guess you noticed they went into the History Department at about eight twenty-five," Rebecca said.

"Yes, and it sounds like they empty the trash in the individual offices each night."

"If they follow that pattern on Wednesday night, we should be alright. I think you'll have to be the lookout man in the foyer while I check out the offices. You can set the redial on your cell phone to my pager number. If you have your phone in your pocket with your finger on the button, you can page me if they start coming into the department before I finish. I'll have my pager on vibrate so they won't hear it go off. If that happens, you'll have to detain them and make a little noise to give me time to close the office door quietly. I'll then walk out, trying to look innocent."

"That should work."

## **Forty-Two**

Wednesday night the three of us met Dr. Chambers and played a few games of pool, trying to act normal and cheerful as if it was just another fun evening. Sarah started doing a few things to get the professor's attention and I sensed she would become a little more overt once they were alone. Rebecca and I left a few minutes before eight, after giving our excuses, and went to the History Department.

I took up my position near the entrance to the department and Rebecca went inside. Her plan was to make a quick survey to make sure there weren't any people in the department. If none were present she would proceed. She didn't come out, so the coast must have been clear. It was one minute after eight.

The sound of a vacuum cleaner was coming from the Sociology Department and I took some comfort feeling the cleaning people were still there as expected. I was trying to look like a curious student reviewing the materials posted on the bulletin board closest to the History Department entrance. Hopefully, I would appear innocent to any passerby, but, inside, I was so tense I couldn't think clearly. I worried what I might do or say if someone tried to enter the department while Rebecca was searching the offices.

My knees felt so weak they could hardly support my one hundred and seventy pounds. If Rebecca didn't finish soon, I was afraid I might collapse.

The elevator bell rang and I heard the door open. Danger. I glanced over my shoulder and an older male student, probably a graduate student, was walking toward me. My pulse raced. I was about to detain him when he veered to a bulletin board to my left. He didn't seem interested in me and I didn't make eye contact. He examined a notice for a minute, tore a tab from the bottom and put it into his pocket. I think he must have known what he was after, since he then left and got back on the elevator. When the elevator door closed, I partially regained my composure, but was still flooded with anxiety.

The sound of the vacuum cleaner ceased. It was twelve minutes after eight. In a few moments a man started to emerge from the Sociology Department. He stopped at the entrance and called back inside, "We're a little ahead of schedule tonight and should be able to go home early. I'll start in the History Department while you finish up here."

My head started spinning. He was much too early. As he left the Sociology Department pushing his cart, I pushed the redial button on my phone to warn Rebecca.

The man moving toward me was about sixty and, since he was approaching me at an angle, I could see a big "Chicago" printed on the front of his sweatshirt. My mind abruptly cleared partially. Trying to appear friendly and innocent, I moved in front of the entrance to the History Department and said, "Are you from Chicago?"

"Yes sir," he replied. "Born and raised there, but I've been here for the last fifteen years."

"It's nice to see someone from the Midwest. I'm from Wisconsin," I said, hoping I sounded sincere and fearing he might notice the quiver in my voice.

He seemed impatient, but I persisted, "Do you like the winters here?"

"The winters are nice, but it's pretty hot here in July and August," he replied as he started to push his cart around me.

As I was desperately trying to think of my next comment, Rebecca walked out of the department. She managed to step around us adroitly, as if nothing was out of the ordinary, and continued toward the elevator.

"Well, I've been happy with the climate so far, but miss the snow," I said as my tension subsided. "Nice talking with you," I concluded as I stepped out of his path.

"Take care," he replied, looking annoyed as he pushed his cart into the History Department.

Still trying to appear innocent, I spent another minute looking at the bulletin board, and then left by the elevator.

According to our plan, I went to the snack room in the basement of the library where I knew Rebecca would be waiting.

The room was almost deserted and she was sitting at a table in the corner. She gave me a weak smile, put her hand on mine, and said quietly but excitedly, "Thanks for the warning and for keeping the janitor occupied for me. It looks like they were running ahead of schedule tonight."

"Unfortunately. Are you alright? I was worried about you."

"I'm fine, but I'm still a little keyed up. Did you have any other problems in the foyer?"

"No, but a guy who seemed like a graduate student gave me a little scare. He looked like he was going into the department, but just got something off the bulletin board and left. How did you come out?"

"I was just getting ready to leave Chambers' office when you buzzed me. I didn't get a chance to get into Costanza's office."

"Find anything interesting?" I asked as I leaned closer to her.

"It was a quick search, but I didn't see anything suspicious in his desk or on his shelves. However, there was a very interesting folder in his file cabinet."

"Oh yeah?"

"Yeah. It was labeled 'Trial' and I looked at it for a couple of minutes. The contents were in chronological order starting at the bottom of the file. At the very bottom was an autopsy report on his wife and a bulletin from her funeral service. Then, there were numerous newspaper clippings about the trial. I'd already seen a couple of them on my internet search. Anywhere the names of Dr. Mason, Clayton Brower, Judge Peters or Steve Simmons were mentioned, they were marked with a yellow highlighter. Next came a newspaper clipping of an article about Brower being arrested for a DUI, with his name and 'DUI' highlighted."

"That's interesting."

"It gets more interesting than that," Rebecca said lowering her voice further. "The top part of the file contained newspaper clippings of all of the murders which we have been following, and the victims names were highlighted wherever they appeared. The most compelling thing was the top item in the file. It was a large note card. I'll show you what it looked like," Rebecca said as she pulled a spiral notebook from her backpack.

She drew a rectangle on a blank page and then printed these words on the simulated card:

"Cast of Characters

    Mason   -   Agamemnon
    Brower   -   Suitors
    Peters   -   Tantalus
    Simmons   -   Sisyphus"

I stared at what she had written, then looked at Rebecca and said, "Pretty amazing."

"I thought so."

"What about that?" I said pointing to her notebook.

"The note card looked pretty suspicious to me. If he made out the card before the murders, it represents his plan. If he made the card out after the murders it could represent his tabulation of the murders he had committed."

"Shocking, isn't it?"

"I think so. I'm glad we got thorough that experience without getting caught. I felt like one of those private investigators you see on TV. It got my blood flowing, but I wouldn't want to do that every day."

"You and me both," I replied. It's good to have that behind us.

We continued talking about a variety of things, waiting for Sarah who was planning to meet us at about nine thirty. She arrived a few minutes after that and slumped down at our table.

"That was a workout, but you would have been proud of me," Sarah said. "It went well. I'll fill you in, but first tell me how things went with you."

It was safe to talk quietly since no one was sitting near us. We took several minutes to tell Sarah about our escapade. She was intrigued and asked questions as we went along. Like Rebecca and me, she felt the words on the note card were quite incriminating.

"Well done," Sarah said smiling. "It's too bad you couldn't get into Costanza's office, but maybe that can be done later. However, the more we learn about Chambers, the more he looks like he's the culprit."

"Okay, Cleopatra," Rebecca said. "Now that we've finished our report, tell us about your evening. I'm dying to hear the lurid details."

Sarah smiled broadly and answered, "It wasn't all that lurid. Not yet. It's too early for that. Tonight I focused on building some rapport and making myself seem interesting. I felt quite devious inside, but I don't think it was obvious to him. Up until a few days ago, I was becoming quite fond of him, but now see him in a totally different light."

"I didn't do any probing into the malpractice trial or the murders or anything like that. I didn't want to appear too sensuous, but just enough to get his attention. It worked out like I hoped. He invited me for an early dinner at his apartment on Friday night. I found out he likes to make spaghetti and, when I explained I loved spaghetti, he invited me over to sample his recipe."

"Why am I not surprised?" I said smiling. "How could he not fall into your seductive web?"

Sarah looked at me, tilted her head and fondled her necklace alluringly as she smiled.

"Okay, Miss femme fatale," Rebecca said in mock annoyance. "What else happened?"

"I told him I would drive my car to his apartment but wouldn't be able to stay long since we were going to celebrate my mother's birthday at my house at eight thirty. So, I'll arrive at six thirty and leave about eight. By the way, it really is my mom's birthday that day."

Sarah paused and then continued, "So, keep Friday night open. You guys need to be my back-up team. Here's the address, apartment number, security gate code and his phone number," she said as she wrote a note and handed it to me.

"We can do that, can't we Rebecca?" I asked.

"Of course."

"Okay," Sarah said. "We did well tonight. Are you ready to leave?"

"Yes, but one thing first," Rebecca said. "Ryan, I don't know if you saw Costanza's e-mail yet, but he wants us to come by his office at two o'clock tomorrow to pick up some posters to take around campus. Should I meet you in the foyer outside the History Department a little before then?"

"Sure. I'll see you there. It will be a little like returning to the scene of the crime."

## **Forty-Three**

Rebecca was in the foyer in front of the History Department when I arrived. I felt a slight shiver as I remembered my efforts at delaying the cleaning man not many hours earlier.

Dr. Costanza's door was open and he was speaking loudly to someone. As we peered into his office, his back was toward us and he was having a lively phone conversation with someone.

"…yes, the fourth murder was the last one and it involved the newspaper reporter," Dr. Costanza said. He then was silent and we couldn't hear the other side of the conversation.

Rebecca and I stiffened a bit and glanced at each other quizzically.

"I know," Dr. Costanza replied to the unseen person on the other end of the line. "What?"…"Okay, well, as I said earlier, this is a perfect follow-up to my two papers on the violence component in Greek myths and legends."

I stepped back toward the reception area away from Dr. Costanza's doorway and motioned for Rebecca to join me. I was fascinated and wanted to hear more of the conversation. Due to the layout of the department, neither the receptionist nor anyone else could see us standing in the hallway. There were some other sounds coming through open office doorways but we could still clearly hear Dr. Costanza's side of the conversation.

I whispered to Rebecca, "Let's just listen until he's done. Act bored while we wait." I looked at my watch. It was just two o'clock.

"Yes, each one ties back. There are direct parallels to Agamemnon, Penelope's suitors, Tantalus, and, my favorite, Sisyphus," Dr. Costanza said.

He paused as he listened and then said, "Thanks. I know. It will get me back in the limelight. I don't want anyone to forget that I exist," he said with a chuckle. "While these are gruesome events, I hate to say it, but it's almost like a dream come true for me to have something like this to write about. What a great way to substantiate my earlier postulates."

He was silent and then wrapped up the conversation saying, "Thanks for your encouraging words, Sam, but let's not get too carried away. It's a little early for too much celebration. But, in our publish or perish world, every little bit helps."

Dr. Costanza was silent again, listening, and then said, "Great. Say hi to Loren. I'll meet you for dinner at your hotel at seven. Bye."

Rebecca raised her eyebrows when I looked at her. It was a habit of hers which I really liked, maybe because it accentuated her beautiful dark eyes. I think she was as surprised as I was at what we had just heard. I looked at my watch and saw it was three minutes after two as we walked to Dr. Costanza's doorway.

His back was to us and he was looking out the window.

I knocked lightly and said, "Dr. Costanza, may we come in?"

He swung his chair around and said in a friendly voice, "Ryan and Rebecca. I guess you received my e-mail. Thanks for coming. Please sit down for a minute."

"Did you have some posters you wanted us to put up?" Rebecca asked politely, as if everything was as normal as ever.

"Yes I do," he replied. "Our next guest lecturer is Sam Berry. He's a brilliant historian and we've been good friends for years. As a matter of fact, I just got off the phone with him. I'll be having dinner with him while he's in town. Here are the posters."

Dr. Costanza seemed to be in an uncharacteristically euphoric mood. He asked us a few things about our classes and then thanked us for continuing to help publicize the guest lecturer series.

Before distributing the posters, we went to the student center to discuss the phone conversation we had just witnessed.

"What did you make of the phone conversation?" I asked Rebecca.

"That's a great question. I wish we could have heard the other side of it as well."

"That would have been nice, but what did you think based on what you heard?"

"Well, we already know he has written some papers about violence in the ancient Greek culture. It must be something which he is known for."

"That's the way it sounded to me. What else do you think?"

"He must be writing a paper on the four murders and seems excited about how they relate to his earlier papers," Rebecca said. "I gathered he feels he will get some good publicity amongst his peers due to this new paper."

"Right. It's almost like the murders are some type of lucky break for him."

"Yes. The question is, was he just lucky the murders occurred or did he commit the murders to provide the basis for his paper?"

"That's exactly what's going through my mind, although a person would have to be pretty desperate for publicity in order to kill four people. So, while Chambers looks like the prime suspect, Costanza could also be a suspect."

"True," Rebecca responded. "They both are experts on ancient Greece and they both have possible motives for committing the murders, although, it seems to me Chambers certainly has the most compelling motive."

"That's a good summary. Isn't it weird? Here we are, college freshmen. We're supposed to be acting like students, not private investigators. Not only that, but we feel one of our professors is guilty of killing four people. We just don't know which one. Is there something wrong with this picture?"

That evening all of the pressures I was facing really started bothering me. My daily updates from my dad about my mom had not been encouraging. Her condition remained poor. She had always been so healthy and I was shocked at how fragile her life now seemed. Every day I kept hoping for encouraging signs, but every day my anxiety increased when she failed to improve.

To make matters worse, I was really getting behind with my studies and I wasn't finding time to practice with our band. Also, I continued to worry about the threatening note I'd received. All of these things, combined with our crime-solving efforts, were taking a toll on my powers of concentration.

## **Forty-Four**

At lunch on Friday, Rebecca and I told Sarah about Dr. Costanza's phone conversation. Her reaction was the same as ours. We still saw Dr. Chambers as the prime suspect and decided to worry about Costanza if we ever ruled out Chambers.

After the Costanza discussion Sarah said, "Let's review our plans for tonight. I'll go to Chambers' apartment at six thirty and you two should get there just after me. Please park near my car and just wait for me in Ryan's car until I leave about eight. Make sure your cell phones are charged and Rebecca has her pager along. I'll have my phone set to ring her pager using redial if I need your help. If you get a page from my phone, knock on the door to see what's going on. If, I need to talk to you, I'll call Rebecca's cell number. If you need to talk to me, call my cell phone. If something unexpected comes up, punt."

"Are you okay with this, Sarah?" I asked.

"Sure," Sarah said sounding confident. "I think I can handle myself. I've had some training in self-defense and always have some pepper spray in my purse.

"So, assuming all goes well, you'll see me get in my car and drive out about eight. I'll then head to my parents' house," Sarah continued. "You can wait a couple minutes so it doesn't look like we were together and then leave yourselves. I'll give you a call for a quick update while we're driving."

"Sounds like a good plan," Rebecca said.

"It should work just fine," Sarah said. "We'll meet in the student center tomorrow morning at ten to decide what to do next. I may try to arrange a date with Chambers for tomorrow night. If so, that would be a good time for you to search his apartment."

Rebecca and I arrived at the apartment complex a little after six thirty and I parked near Sarah's relic. Its dents weren't very obvious in the darkness. There were many buildings in the complex and the parking lots were almost full. We were between a mini van and a SUV and Rebecca and I were not very visible from most vantage points. I doubt we would have looked suspicious to anyone who may have noticed us.

We passed the time talking quietly and hoped Sarah was safe inside the apartment. The complex was quite luxurious. I had noticed a large pool, activities building and tennis courts as we drove in.

We kept getting more nervous as the time passed but finally were very relieved when we saw Sarah get into her car just after eight, right on schedule. She drove toward the main gate. We followed in the same direction a few minutes later.

As we were pulling out of the gate, Rebecca's phone rang and she talked briefly with Sarah.

"Sarah's in good spirits," Rebecca said with relief. "She feels it was worthwhile and our assignment is still on for tomorrow night. She'll tell us everything when we get together in the morning."

We met at ten on Saturday morning as planned. Sarah was upbeat and Rebecca and I were anxious to hear her report.

"I'd give myself an A for my performance last night if grades were being assigned," Sarah said excitedly. "It actually would have been an enjoyable date if it wasn't for our underlying sinister plan. Chambers was pleasant and well-behaved and his spaghetti was quite respectable as well."

"I wish I could have seen you in action," Rebecca said. "Did you turn on your charms?"

"Of course, but I didn't go overboard. I need to play a little hard to get for awhile until we see how this pans out. Anyway, he's starting to feel pretty comfortable with me and I was able to get him to loosen up and say some things he probably wouldn't have mentioned under other circumstances."

"Like what?" I asked.

"I got him talking about his wife, her unexpected death and the malpractice trial. He was devastated when she died and blamed Dr. Mason. In terms of the trial, he felt Mason lied in court and was backed up by some expert witnesses. There was a question as to whether or not one of those witnesses should have been able to testify, and that person's testimony was particularly supportive of Mason. In any event, Judge Peters decided to allow the witness to testify. Chambers' biggest disappointment, however, was with his attorney, Clayton Brower, whom he felt made many serious blunders in the trial. While he had already told us some of this, last night his hatred toward Mason, Brower and Peters was very evident."

"That's interesting," I said. "Did he say anything about Steve Simmons?"

"Not at first. But, when he finished venting about these three men and the trial in general he said the media coverage, particularly as reported by Simmons, was very biased and in support of Dr. Mason."

"After hearing all of this, do you feel he hated these men enough to actually murder them?" Rebecca asked seriously.

"I really feel he wanted revenge and would consider murder justifiable."

"So, you think he would consider murder justifiable," I said. "Do you think he actually committed the murders?"

"I felt that way before last night, and I feel further convinced now. You'd feel the same way if you heard him go through all of that last night."

"But," Sarah said changing the subject. "I certainly didn't want the whole evening to be on the trial and related matters. We talked about many lighter subjects and I ended up with another date with him tonight. We're going to try out the new Mexican restaurant near campus."

"Charming," Rebecca said.

"Yeah," Sarah replied. "And your assignment should be fairly simple. I'm sure you must have noticed that his apartment is on the first floor. The good thing is that it has a ground level patio on the back of the building. He showed the patio to me and I noticed it's pretty well obscured by a railing and bushes. You should be able to slip into the apartment after dark through the patio door without being seen. When Chambers was in the bathroom, I unlocked the door. Therefore you will be able walk right in, unless he happened to lock the door after I left. He probably won't notice it's unlocked since he says he never used the patio."

"Your resourcefulness continues to amaze me," I said approvingly.

"Thanks," Sarah replied.

Sarah then got a piece of paper and pencil from her backpack and drew a sketch showing us how to find the patio for Chambers' apartment. She also sketched the layout of the rooms and furniture in the apartment.

"There," Sarah said. "That will be of help to you."

"What time is your dinner tonight?" I asked Sarah.

"I'm meeting him at the restaurant at seven thirty and mentioned I would have to leave by nine thirty in order to get back to campus to meet some friends."

"Okay," I said, "We'll go into his apartment about seven forty-five and probably won't stay for more than thirty minutes. With two of us we can make a fairly thorough search in that amount of time."

"I'll wear my best cat burglar outfit," Rebecca said smiling slyly as she made a purring sound.

"Good idea," I said.

"Okay, you two," Sarah said in mock seriousness. "This is all business tonight, not pleasure. We need to keep focused on our mission."

"We'll do our best, commander," Rebecca said with a cute salute back to Sarah.

"Thank you," Sarah replied. "Let's meet back in the library snack room at nine forty-five tonight to compare notes."

## **Forty-Five**

I parked near the patio for Chambers' apartment at seven forty-seven according to the clock on the dash of my Cavalier. It was dark and the area around the patio was not well lit. I was encouraged by those conditions and expected we would be able to slip through the patio door, assuming it was still unlocked, without being noticed. If Chambers had locked it, I felt Rebecca would know how to open the door. A man and woman walked to a car near us. As we waited for them to leave, I reached over and squeezed Rebecca's hand and said quietly, "Are you ready for this?"

"I'm ready," she said as she squeezed back.

"The coast is clear, let's go before anyone else comes."

"First, let's put these on," Rebecca said as she gave me a pair of thin latex gloves.

I looked at her approvingly. We slipped on our gloves and got out of the car. I felt like a criminal about to strike, but assured myself we were doing the right thing.

We walked the short distance to the patio, took a quick look around, saw no people and then climbed over the low railing onto the patio. I slowly touched the door and was relieved when the knob turned smoothly. The door pushed inward with minimal effort. I closed it and could make out a lamp near the door in the faint light coming in from the parking lot. I turned it on. We were in the living room and could see the kitchen and small dining area. We knew the location of the two bedrooms from Sarah's sketch.

Despite the anxiety I was feeling, I couldn't help noticing how striking Rebecca looked, all in black, in her snug sweater, leather pants and sneakers. She looked like a lead actress from a James Bond movie.

"You weren't kidding about your outfit. You look great."

"I'm glad you like it," Rebecca replied tensely. "I felt it might help if I dressed for the occasion."

We walked over close to the entrance. I turned on another light and said, "Ok, let's get this over with as soon as we can. You check the bedrooms and I'll check the living room, kitchen and dining area."

"Roger."

Just then we heard noise coming from outside the front door and a key being inserted into the lock. We glanced at each other with looks of panic and my heart raced.

The person at the door was trying to turn the key but it wasn't turning. The key was removed and reinserted and tried again. We were frozen and couldn't move. I was about ready to grab Rebecca and scramble out the patio door when we heard a man say loudly. "He said one-twenty-four didn't he?"

A woman replied, "Maybe it was two-twenty-four. Let's try the one right above this one."

We sighed with relief as we heard the key being pulled from the lock.

"That scared the hell out of me," Rebecca whispered loudly.

"You and me both," I replied feeling the tension subside. "Let's get on with it."

I looked through drawers, cabinets and closets and checked all of the book shelves. Nothing looked unusual until I came to one bookshelf which contained numerous mystery novels and four books on serial killers.

Just as I was finishing, Rebecca stepped into the living room and motioned me into one of the bedrooms which was fixed up like a study.

She slid open the top right hand drawer in the desk and said, "Look at this."

There was a snub-nosed revolver, a box of ammunition and some loose bullets in the drawer. We didn't touch them, but stared at them for a few seconds before Rebecca closed the drawer.

She then slid open the center desk drawer, pulled out a scratch pad and laid it on the desk top.

"Now, look at this," She said excitedly.

The following words were neatly printed on the top page of the pad:

> **"Mary,**
>
> **Your tormentors are now all gone.**
> **Rest in peace, my love.**
> **Your husband forever,**
>
> **James"**

"That's really something. I'm going to write that down," I said as I pulled a sheet of paper and a pen from my pocket and wrote out a copy of the note.

"Did you find anything else in here or in his bedroom?" I asked.

"No. How about you?"

"Just some books. Come, I'll show you."

I showed Rebecca the mystery and serial killer books and I wrote down the titles and authors of the latter on my sheet of paper.

We turned off all of the lights and I locked the door to the patio before I quietly pulled it shut. As we stepped onto the patio we heard voices in the parking lot and crouched down to stay out of sight. The voices belonged to three young men who got into a pick up truck and drove away.

Once they were gone it seemed quiet. We then eased ourselves over the railing and walked to my car, trying to seem inconspicuous. I remained quite tense until we had driven out of the apartment complex.

"We made it," Rebecca said. "I've had about enough of this sort of thing for awhile."

"Me too. I can see now that I'm not cut out for this type of work."

Rebecca and I met Sarah as planned at nine forty-five. Sarah was anxious to hear our report before she told us about her date, so we took a few minutes to fill her in. Then I showed her my paper containing the note Chambers had written to his departed wife and the information on the serial killer books.

"Good work," Sarah said when Rebecca and I had finished talking about our mission. "That must have given you quite a scare when the man tried to get into the apartment."

"Tell me about it!" Rebecca responded.

"The gun, the note to his wife and the serial killer books further point to his probable guilt," Sarah said.

"How did your evening go?" I asked Sarah.

"It went fine. Nothing special happened. I didn't learn anything new but concentrated on trying to elevate his romantic interests up another level.

"I assume there is a reason behind this." I said to Sarah.

"Well, I'm not doing it for the fun of it. But, my main weapon, so to speak, is being a member of the opposite sex. I can use that as a tool in confirming his guilt or innocence. Sometimes you have to exploit all of your assets."

"All of this is making me nervous, but I guess you know what you are doing," I said.

"I'm not too damn calm about this either, but think I know what I'm doing," Sarah replied. "By the way, I think it's time for us to talk to the police again and let them know what we've found out."

"Ryan, do you think they'll take us seriously if we see them again?" Rebecca asked.

"Probably. They told us to let them know if we came up with new information. I think we've got some things to say that will get their attention."

"Before we talk to the police, however, we must get our story and facts well organized," Sarah said. "For example, we can't tell them exactly how we got some of the information. I suggest we all think about this for the next day or so and plan our strategy with the police over lunch on Monday."

As we were getting ready to leave, Sarah eyed Rebecca for a couple of seconds and said as she smiled approvingly, "Hey girl, you really did dress for the part tonight. You could get poor Ryan pretty excited dressing like that. I hope he behaved himself."

## **Forty-Six**

Sunday night after leaving the library about ten, I went to the dorm. As I approached my room, I noticed a brown paper bag on the floor in front of the door. "**Ryan Anderson**" was neatly printed on the side of the bag facing me. I tensed a bit and hoped this was nothing sinister. I scanned the hallway in both directions, but no one was in sight.

I opened the door with my key, reached in and turned on the light. I peered carefully into the room, looked in the closets, under the beds, and, after finding no one, I picked up the bag and closed the door.

Mike was not home and I was thankful for that. The bag was heavy for its size and it was folded shut. I slowly unfolded the bag and carefully looked inside. It contained a white box which looked like it may have held a new watch at one time. I held the box at arms length and opened it very slowly.

There was a rock wrapped in a piece of white paper in the box. I tensed up on seeing the rock, which looked like it could have been white marble, and then looked at the paper. It contained a typewritten message in bold print which read:

> "**Simmons got two of these in his final days.**
> **Stop putting your nose where it doesn't belong or**
> **you will end up just like him.**"

I immediately felt sick and almost threw up. When I had gotten the envelope under my door earlier, I was concerned, but now I was really scared. Although both the envelope and the bag could have been left by a practical joker, I feared the worst and concluded the person behind the murders must have left the threats.

This didn't look good. Somehow the killer, be that Dr. Chambers or someone else, must know I was investigating the murders and was apparently trying to get me to back off. If he was after me, maybe he would also come after Rebecca and Sarah.

Not knowing what else to do, I put everything back in the bag and stuffed it into my backpack, undressed and got into bed.

I was now firmly convinced we needed to go to the police as soon as possible. Trying to get any sleep was hopeless. I later heard Mike come in and go to bed, but I pretended to be asleep. Exhaustion eventually overpowered my anxiety and I dozed off for the last part of the night.

"Let me tell you the latest," I said as we started eating our lunch the next morning. After checking to make sure we weren't being closely observed, I showed Rebecca and Sarah the paper bag and its contents.

"Ryan, this is all getting pretty scary," Rebecca said.

"At first, when I got the envelope, I felt it could have just been a practical joke. Now, I'm convinced these things came from the murderer. It's getting me stressed out."

"If Chambers is behind these threats, it's like he is trying to stop you from investigating the murders," Sarah said. "We told him earlier that we were trying to help the police."

"Right," I replied. "If I'm being threatened, you two could be next."

"Yeah," Rebecca said with a worried look on her face.

"On Saturday night we agreed it would be wise to re-contact the police," Sarah said. "That is now a must. Let's call Lieutenant Waters now and try to set up a meeting as soon as possible."

"Should we do that or would it be wise for us to just back off and let the police deal with everything?" Rebecca asked tentatively. She then looked at the expressions on our faces and said, "I didn't think so."

"Okay, here goes," I said, having fished Lieutenant Waters' card from my backpack. I dialed his number on my cell phone and had to wait about two minutes while someone got him to the phone. I gave him a quick recap of why we needed to meet with him. He was initially noncommittal, but eventually agreed to meet with us at three o'clock the next day.

Lieutenant Waters ushered us into the conference room. Lieutenant Grimes and Sergeant Henderson were again present. Lieutenant Waters asked me to give a detailed explanation of what had transpired since our last meeting. I went into depth explaining most of the things we had learned and how we had concluded Dr. Chambers was the likely murderer of the four victims.

I explained how we had gotten to know Chambers quite well on a social basis and, due to that, had become aware of certain suspicious items in his office and home. I didn't say anything about our breaking and entering exploits or our scheme to learn more about Chambers through Sarah's counterfeit romantic efforts. Sarah did mention she had been on some dates with Dr. Chambers and that some of our intelligence arose out of those encounters. I was relieved when the detectives didn't press me as to how we became aware of the items in Chambers' office and home. For all they knew, he may have revealed these things on his own initiative.

Their level of interest increased when I told of the two threats I had received. While I did most of the talking, Sarah and Rebecca both made some convincing points which supported my comments.

The detectives asked a few questions while the three of us were giving our views, but most of their questions were asked after we were done talking. By the time they finished asking questions, it was clear to me the detectives felt, as we did, that Chambers was a prime suspect, at least in terms of the Brower, Peters and Simmons murders.

Lieutenant Grimes concluded that we needed to find a way to clearly determine if Dr. Chambers was guilty. In response to his comments, Sarah outlined a plan, albeit one which put her at some personal risk. It was very controversial, but it was eventually decided to give it a try if the proper ground work could be laid in advance.

Later that night I wasn't very successful focusing on my studies and kept thinking about our plan. The idea was for Sarah to get Chambers to meet her in room one-twenty in Davis Hall at ten o'clock Friday night, a time when no one would be expected to disturb them. She would tell him the room had a symbolic significance since it was where our Greek mythology class was held and she wanted to use that special setting to convey an important message to him.

In the room that evening, she would tell him she had fallen in love with him and wanted to consummate their relationship in the classroom. As she was getting him aroused, she would tell him she felt he was guilty of the murders, but wanted him to know she didn't care since she was convinced that his reasons for the murders were clearly justified as his final tribute to his beloved wife. We expected he would be enthralled with her actions and would confess to the crimes while smothered in her embraces.

The police would be hidden in the studio which opened into the classroom where they would record the confession and then charge in and arrest Chambers before anything further happened. We had convinced the police he was guilty, and they agreed to participate in this trap. If Chambers did not confess to the murders, Sarah would act surprised and cool her emotions as gracefully as possible under the circumstances. If she could not safely free herself, the police would be there to protect her.

The campus police would be brought in on the scheme. Sarah had insisted that Rebecca and I be allowed to hide with the police in the studio, and, much to my surprise, they had reluctantly agreed.

When Sarah had suggested this plan during our meeting with Lieutenant Waters and his partners, I had been initially shocked at her proposal, as had Rebecca and the detectives. But, as Sarah methodically outlined her complete plan, and had ready answers to our questions, we all eventually felt the plan, while almost fanciful, was an effective strategy to follow. We were convinced she possessed the romantic and acting talents necessary for the plan to succeed. Any outside observer would probably have thought we were out of our minds.

While Waters and his men were only handling one of the murder investigations, it sounded like they would coordinate with the officials involved in the other three cases.

The first phase of the plan was to take place on Wednesday night. Rebecca and I would have an excuse for leaving the pool game early.

When she was alone with Dr. Chambers, Sarah would carefully entice him into meeting her in the classroom on Friday night.

Sarah artfully started weaving her web even before Rebecca and I excused ourselves from the pool game. She was amazing to watch. By the time Rebecca and I made our exit, Sarah had Chambers under her spell. They hardly noticed us leave.

I had no doubt that, by the end of the evening, Chambers would be so mesmerized he would be powerless to avoid meeting Sarah on Friday night.

Friday, Rebecca, Sarah and I met for lunch. Sarah was confident the trap had been effectively set. Chambers would meet her that night as we had hoped. We reviewed the details of the plan and, just as Sarah was about to make a final point, I saw Tyler approaching.

He walked to the empty chair at our table and asked, "Mind if I join you?"

"Not at all, Tyler," I said. "What's going on? We haven't talked to you for awhile."

Tyler put his drink on the table and shifted his backpack to his lap as he sat down. Then, he smiled and said cheerfully, "Couldn't be better. It seems like everything has been going my way lately. How are you all enjoying Dr. Chambers' class this term?"

"He's doing a good job," Rebecca said. "I like it even better than his class last semester."

"So do I," Sarah added. "What do you think, Tyler?"

"It's pretty interesting, but sometimes I wish he would go into a little more depth with some of the key characters."

Tyler took a sip from his drink and was about to continue talking when he started coughing loudly. He bent over to regain his composure and coughed a few times before sitting upright.

"Sorry," Tyler said apologetically, "That went down the wrong way. Anyway, Chambers knows his stuff and it's a good class." His voice was still raspy as he said, after coughing again, "I have a very sore throat, and it doesn't take much to set off a coughing jag. If you'll excuse me, I think I'll get some fresh air. See you later."

Once Tyler was out of earshot, Sarah continued by saying, "So, as I was about to conclude before Tyler joined us, everything is all set.

*Alan Beske*

My rendezvous will be at ten tonight in room one-twenty Davis Hall. I can't wait for the police to learn what's really going on."

## **Forty-Seven**

Sarah, Rebecca and I entered room one-twenty at nine thirty, along with Lieutenant Waters, Lieutenant Grimes, Sergeant Henderson, two armed campus officers and a technician who was sworn to secrecy.

Someone flipped on the lights. I had spent many daytime hours there in class, but felt uneasy being present at this odd hour. The bright lights didn't do much to give me comfort.

A cabinet containing computer and projection equipment was centered on the large lecture floor. The semi-circular rows of auditorium-style seats looked like they would hold up to one hundred and fifty students. The classroom was occasionally used for video conferences and was equipped with microphones and TV cameras. A recording studio, hidden behind a one-way mirror, could be entered from the classroom through a sound-proof door.

Sarah stayed on the lecture floor and the rest of us went into the studio. It was cold in there and the lights were dim. I noticed Rebecca shivering as the technician focused the video cameras, turned on the microphones, did sound checks, and started the VCR's. We could see the images from each camera on a bank of monitors.

Everything was ready. We waited in silence, broken only by a few whispered comments. Sarah paced nervously and the sensitive microphones captured the hollow clicks of her loafers on the tile floor. The close-up camera revealed the strained expression on her face. The faint fragrance of Rebecca's perfume mingled with the musty smell of the studio as she brushed against me, but my stomach continued to churn.

Much to my surprise, when the door from the hallway to the classroom opened, the person who entered was Tyler Sanders. Not Dr. Chambers. I noticed by the digital clock in the studio that it was nine forty-one.

Sarah tensed when the door opened and a surprised look came across her face when she saw Tyler.

Tyler slowly walked toward Sarah and stopped about five feet from her. He made a wry smile and said, "Sarah, we have something important to discuss." His hands were in the pockets of his bulky green windbreaker.

Everyone in the studio pushed closer to the one-way mirror.

"Tyler!" Sarah said excitedly. "What are you doing here?"

"The question really is, what are you doing here so early? I planned to get here before you."

"What are you talking about?" Sarah exclaimed.

"I'm talking about this," Tyler said as he pulled a small object from his left jacket pocket and thrust it toward Sarah.

Sarah's recorded voice came from the object which was some type of recording device, "My rendezvous will be at ten tonight in room one-twenty Davis Hall. I can't wait for the police to learn what's really going on."

Sarah stiffened, and in a quivering voice said, "Where did you get that?"

"It's amazing what marvels you can find on the spy equipment web sites," Tyler said menacingly, "During my little coughing fit this morning, I stuck this jewel under your table. After you left, I eavesdropped on what you said."

"Why would you do that? Why are you staring at me like that? You're scaring me, Tyler."

"You and your two friends are sticking your noses where they don't belong. You're trying to solve murders that don't need to be solved because the victims all deserved to die."

"What are you saying?" Sarah said with a look of revelation and fear spreading across her face.

"I think you're getting the picture," Tyler answered shrilly. "I was justified in killing all four of them and now they can't harm anyone else. Whatever you had planned to tell the police will die with your beautiful body tonight."

Tyler slowly pulled his right hand from his jacket pocket and pointed a pistol at Sarah's face. She lunged sideways.

"Freeze...police!" shouted Lieutenant Waters bursting into the classroom followed by his fellow officers and the two campus policemen, all with their guns drawn.

Sarah dove behind the equipment cabinet, putting it between her and Tyler.

Tyler reeled around and faced the officers with his gun raised and pointed above their heads. The startled look on his face melted and a devious smile took its place.

"Drop that gun!" shouted Lieutenant Waters.

Rebecca and I stared in disbelief through the one-way mirror. My heart pounded.

"Surprise, surprise," Tyler said defiantly with remarkable steadiness as he raised his arms, still holding the gun. "You leave me no choice gentlemen." He whirled around, fired in Sarah's direction, pulled a second pistol from his jacket pocket with his left hand, and dived on the floor where he was shielded from the officers under the front row of seats.

Tyler then fired toward the officers and toward Sarah again. Two of his shots tore into the equipment cabinet and one crashed into the one-way mirror inches above Rebecca and me, showering us with pieces of glass. There was a deafening roar as all five officers fired back at Tyler while they scattered and hid behind seats. Tyler kept alternating his fire between the officers and Sarah.

Rebecca and I dropped to the floor and peered through the remains of the one-way mirror. Bullets ricocheted with piercing screams off the hard walls and floors and my ears ached from the thunderous blasts and echoes. Concrete dust and debris from the ceiling filled the air. A suspended microphone plunged to the floor, the face of a wall clock exploded and the hands from the clock spiraled downward like a crippled helicopter.

I felt the wind from a bullet which missed my head by centimeters and obliterated a VCR behind me. I doubled over and nearly barfed while Rebecca shrieked. The technician was screaming violently from under a desk, but I could barely hear her over the gunfire. I raised my left hand toward the side of my head and felt a sharp pain as another bullet flew by catching the edge of my hand.

It hurt like hell and was bleeding.

The mayhem continued for at least a minute as the officers kept Tyler pinned down under the seats, but then he broke for the exit, dodging and slipping, leaving a trail of blood. Two well-placed rounds slammed him into the front wall to the right of the door to the hall. His body seemed frozen briefly, then slowly slid down to a near sitting position, with arms limp and legs splayed grotesquely. Red streaks on the beige concrete blocks traced his body's descent.

All firing stopped abruptly and the technician choked off her screams.

Sarah sobbed wildly near the equipment cabinet where she squatted in a tight ball with her hands forcing her head into her lap.

Four of the officers inched toward Tyler holding their guns pointed at him with both hands. They were ready to fire if he showed any movement. Sergeant Henderson was bent over and there was blood on his neck.

Rebecca and I crept out of the studio and slipped behind the officers as they cautiously moved forward. They were so fixated on Tyler they didn't notice or stop us. Rebecca had glass fragments in her hair and blood trickled down her forehead.

As we approached Tyler, I saw one of the campus policemen lying on his side holding his leg. Sarah, still sobbing, now more quietly, rose shakily to her feet and stumbled toward me, arms crossed tightly across her chest, as she warily focused her eyes on Tyler. Much of the beauty had drained from her face. When she reached me she laced an arm through mine and pressed against me.

I smelled the gun smoke, but it was barely visible. A drop of sweat made me shiver as it rolled down my side under my shirt. Some glass from the one-way mirror fell and broke the silence when it hit the hard floor.

Tyler's eyes were closed and he was not moving, except for his chest as he struggled for air. Blood oozed from his open mouth and bullet holes in his chest and leg. His two guns lay on the floor near his open hands.

The officers were braced for action and kept their guns trained on Tyler.

Tyler straightened his head slightly, his eyes fluttered open and he muttered in a labored voice, "They put my brother in prison for something he didn't do." He paused as more blood seeped from his lips and continued in a barely audible voice. "Now he has been avenged."

The officers were poised to shoot, but held their fire.

Tyler coughed with a horrifying gurgling sound and his eyes closed. Moments later, his shoulders convulsed and his body rolled slowly to the side. His head hit the floor with a sickening thud. All bodily motions stopped, save for two drops of blood which dripped from his mouth. The expression on his face was surprisingly peaceful.

Lieutenant Waters then knelt and held his fingers on Tyler's carotid artery for several moments. The other officers kept their guns trained on Tyler as they crouched with their knees bent. Waters then said, "He's dead."

Tension dropped as the officers lowered their guns and returned them to their holsters. The standing campus policeman rushed to help his partner.

My hand was still burning and dripping blood, but I could tell the wound wasn't serious. I put my arms around Rebecca and Sarah and pulled the three of us together. I knew I was bleeding on Rebecca's shoulder, but that seemed unimportant. They were sobbing softly. We stood like that for a minute or two, then slumped into chairs in the first row. I vaguely felt some wood splinters from bullet holes pushing against my back, but I ignored the mild pain. It was somehow comforting. My hand was throbbing but the pain was diminishing.

The wounded campus police officer and Sergeant Henderson sat propped against the wall and seemed to be in pain. However, they were talking quietly and their injuries didn't appear to be life-threatening.

I was between Rebecca and Sarah and they were holding my arms tightly. They both were trembling and my ears were still ringing while Lieutenant Waters requested three ambulances on his cell phone. He then called someone and ordered investigators to the crime scene.

*Alan Beske*

The studio technician, looking very pale and nervous, sat in a seat off to our left. She came out of the studio after Tyler had been killed.

The door to the classroom opened and Dr. Chambers peered in. His jaw dropped. Lieutenant Grimes quickly pushed him back into the hallway.

Lieutenant Waters closed his cell phone and surveyed Rebecca, Sarah and me. "Are any of you hurt?"

His voice brought me back to reality and away from the gruesome sights and sounds which were playing back in my mind and I said, "Just a nick," as I showed him my hand.

"Nothing serious," Rebecca said, just above a whisper.

"I'm okay," Sarah added is a parched voice. Miraculously, she had not been hurt, even though the cabinet which gave her shelter was mangled by several bullets Tyler had meant for her.

"Good," he replied. "Just to be sure, we'll have the paramedics look at you when they get here."

While we were awaiting the paramedics and crime scene personnel, Lieutenant Waters questioned us and the studio technician and tried to calm all of us down. Slowly, my adrenaline level dropped and I started thinking more clearly.

Lieutenant Grimes had not yet returned. I assumed he was questioning Dr. Chambers.

The paramedics and other people were soon in the room. The paramedics, after they attended to Tyler, and the injured officers, examined Rebecca, Sarah and me. They cleaned and bandaged Rebecca's and my wounds and said police reports would be filed concerning our injuries. I was told to get stitches in my hand at our university hospital emergency room when the police had finished with us.

Tyler's body was left in place and the injured officers were removed on stretchers.

We were questioned by various people and in between questioners watched the crime scene investigators perform their grisly tasks. They were thankful video tapes had captured the bizarre spectacle. I hoped I would never have to view those tapes. Going through this once was enough for me.

Lieutenant Grimes eventually returned to the room, but Dr. Chambers was not with him.

The studio technician was allowed to leave and about thirty minutes later the three of us were released by Lieutenant Waters around midnight. He said we would be hearing more from them soon.

Out front on the sidewalk, Rebecca exclaimed, "That was horrible. Thank God we survived...Sarah, how awful for you..."

"I'm still shaking. I can't believe he missed me. Next time I see one of those cabinets, I'm giving it a big hug," she said trying to laugh, but not succeeding.

"Bullets were flying everywhere. Amazing no one else got hurt," I said feeling somewhat revived by the cool air.

"It was like being in a war zone," Rebecca said.

"Yeah, with thundering sound effects and splinters in my clothes," Sarah responded. "Too real for me."

"Can you believe it?" I blurted, "Tyler killed those guys, not Chambers.! I don't know what he meant about his brother, but I guess somehow that will be sorted out."

"Man, were we wrong!" Rebecca exclaimed.

"More like stupid," Sarah added.

"Hey, you guys, we have nothing to feel bad about," I said. "While we stumbled into it, the crimes were solved because of what we did. Tyler was punished for killing four people and stopped before he killed more."

"You're right there," Sarah said. "I'm not sorry for Tyler. I was almost his next victim."

"Almost, but not quite," Rebecca said as she gave Sarah a long firm hug. "You're okay, we're okay, and those two officers will be fine after a little healing. Tyler was the only one who didn't make it and he deserved what he got."

"Right," Sarah sighed. "I'm wiped out. I need to sleep before I collapse. Ryan, what about your hand?"

"No big deal."

"We'll get you to your room and I'll go with Ryan to the emergency room," Rebecca said. "We'll talk tomorrow."

Sarah smiled weakly and said, "Yeah, y'all. Like Scarlett said, tomorrow's another day."

## **Forty-Eight**

*Many thoughts flashed through Tyler's mind as he lay, mortally wounded, propped against the block wall with his eyes closed. His senses were remarkably keen in his final seconds, although the pain was severe and his body was destroyed. He knew he was about to die. He accepted that and felt no remorse about killing the four men who had been responsible for his brother's incarceration. Imminent death caused no change of heart.*

*He didn't think he'd hit Sarah, although he had sure tried. It would have been an easy task if the policemen hadn't surprised him. What were they doing there so early? Now, it really didn't matter. Sarah was not his main concern. He had carried out his core mission to his full satisfaction.*

*He forced his eyes open and saw the guns pointed at him, but managed to explain his actions before his voice failed and his eyes closed.*

*His pain changed into numbness. His mind clouded for a few moments, turned blank, then ceased to function. Life left him as his shoulders shook and his body slumped to the floor.*

# **Epilogue**

We didn't use room one-twenty Davis Hall for the rest of the semester and finished out our mythology class in a substitute classroom. It was just as well, as far as I was concerned. Maybe some day, after the room was fully restored, I would return to the scene of that awful evening shootout, but I was in no hurry.

Following Tyler's death, his motives became known through police reports and exhaustive media coverage. Two years earlier his brother had been sentenced to life imprisonment for the murder of a person in a barroom brawl. The brother had maintained he acted in self-defense, but the jury had not seen it that way. Tyler's brother's attorney had been Clayton Brower and the quality of Brower's defense efforts was certainly suspect. Dr. Mason had treated the man shot by Tyler's brother before he died and testified for the prosecution. Judge Peters had presided at the trial and Steve Simmons had reported on the trial. It became apparent that Tyler, his convicted brother and his parents had held Brower, Mason, Peters and Simmons responsible for the guilty verdict. Tyler had been exceptionally close to his brother growing up, and set out on his own to seek revenge. No one else was aware of his intentions.

Evidence was found in Tyler's apartment, including a diary, which detailed how he had meticulously planned the four murders and how and why he decided to parallel each murder with a representative character in ancient Greek mythology. Investigators theorized that Tyler had somehow become psychologically deranged, giving rise to his motive and actions, but no facts emerged to back up this assumption.

It was clear from Tyler's diary that he had left the two threats for me and clear that he had planned to kill Sarah in Davis Hall since he assumed she had learned of his guilt and planned to inform the police. He then planned to kill Rebecca and me. His mistaken interpretation of Sarah's recorded remarks had proven deadly.

I've asked myself many times what might have happened if he hadn't made his recording at our lunch table. But, it really doesn't matter. What happened, happened.

There is no use speculating on what might have happened.

Obviously, our suspicion that Dr. Chambers was the murderer, while seemingly very plausible, was totally wrong. The notes and other "evidence," we had found were false clues of an assumed guilt. Fortunately, we had never accused him of being guilty. We were greatly relieved he was innocent.

With all that had happened, Sarah's emotional interest in Dr. Chambers evaporated, but she soon found a new boyfriend on campus to replace the one she had tired of.

Due to a chance encounter, I managed to introduce Dr. Chambers to Jean Wilkins. I wasn't surprised when I saw them having lunch together a few days later. My guess is that they will be seeing more of each other in the future.

My mother, after some additional ups and downs, finally recovered and resumed normal activities. Her frightening ordeal finally ended.

Needless to say, Dr. Costanza, despite some of our earlier theories, had nothing to do with the murders. His personality left something to be desired, but he was no murderer.

All charges were dropped against Burt Atkins. Despite the apologies he received from the police and prosecutors, he filed a lawsuit hoping to get some reward to offset the false claims made against him. He and his wife Lorie have separated. No one was shocked by that.

Monica and I decided to end our relationship. Being apart had caused us both to consider other options. Rebecca and I have been together ever since.

Rebecca's had a little more time for archery lately and blew her competition away at a recent match.

We resumed our Wednesday evening pool games and are getting some enjoyment from that. But, it will be awhile before things get fully back to normal, if they ever do.

Our band keeps getting better and we have two gigs scheduled. I'd rather play my guitar than play detective any day. It may not be as exciting, but it's much less dangerous.

Dr. Chambers told us months ago that knowledge of the past helped us deal with the issues of today. He was right, of course. Had Rebecca, Sarah and I not held to our conviction that ancient Greek legacies provided critical clues, I'm convinced that the perpetrator of four of Atlanta's most heinous crimes may have never been brought to justice.

It has been two months since the blood bath in Davis Hall. After getting over the initial shock, I've been feeling a little better each day. Finals start next week. The required concentration should be therapeutic. All of us are looking forward to putting this painful semester behind us.

## **Author Questions and Answers**

**Q:** This is your first novel. Why did you decide to write a mystery?

**A:** I've always wanted to write a book, although never could discipline myself to start working on one while I was actively engaged in my career. Once I retired, I acquired a nice volume of discretionary time and that made it easy for me to begin. After more than thirty years of business writing, I wanted to try my hand at fiction. Mysteries are my favorite form of fiction, so doing a mystery was a logical choice.

**Q:** Why did you incorporate a Greek mythology theme in *Ancient Legacies Unleashed*?

**A:** I've been interested in the civilization of the ancient Greeks since taking an ancient history class as a college freshman. Their cultural and political accomplishments were remarkable and their legacies have impacted humankind for more than two thousand years. Greek mythology is also fascinating to me. I felt readers might enjoy a story linking certain of these ancient myths and legends to our contemporary society.

**Q:** Is there a reason why you decided to feature college students as your central characters?

**A:** College was a very enjoyable experience for me and I wanted to have the story take place in an academic environment. Furthermore, that seemed to fit nicely with the Greek mythology theme.

**Q:** Is your book aimed at a specific audience, such as college students?

**A:** Not really, but hopefully, it will appeal to college students, former college students and people who plan to attend college. Beyond that, it should be of interest to others, such as people who like mysteries or ancient Greece. Due to the setting, the book may be of particular interest to readers who live in Atlanta or North Georgia.

**Q:** Are any of the characters based on people you have known?

**A:** Not specifically, but perhaps there are some attributes of the characters which have been drawn from people I've known.

**Q:** Your narrator, Ryan Anderson, came from Wisconsin and you're from Minnesota. Are there any parallels between you and Ryan?

**A:** There are some. I came from a small town in Southern Minnesota and Ryan is from a small town in Southwestern Wisconsin. There are also some similarities between us in terms of the adjustment one makes when moving from a sheltered rural setting to an urban university environment.

**Q:** Was it difficult to move from business writing to fiction?

**A:** There is a definite learning curve when it comes to writing fiction, and writing a mystery specifically. I've never had any training in creative writing and that was a handicap. However, I learned some things in this first effort which will help me in the future.

**Q:** How long did it take you to write *Ancient Legacies Unleashed*?

**A:** I wrote the first draft in four months. After that, I worked on revisions intermittently, with some lengthy pauses, for another eleven months before it was completed.

**Q:** Are you working on another book now?

**A:** I've started a new novel. It's about a reclusive billionaire who kidnaps some people with specialized talents for the purpose of carrying out a mysterious mission.

## **About the Author**

Alan Beske grew up in Minnesota and received undergraduate and graduate degrees from the University of Minnesota. After college, he began a business career which took him and his family to many locations in the United States before moving to the Atlanta area in the 1980's. He and his wife moved to the mountains of North Georgia following his retirement. This is his first novel.

Printed in the United States
36531LVS00003B/220-231